The Anderssen Gambit

By B J Pascal

ISBN: 1942393008

ISBN 13: 978-1-942393-00-9

When he sees his agency turning to more and more sinister methods to control the country, Henry Fletcher seeks the help of foreign services and retired CIA agent David Monthausser to straighten the agency's course. In the process, Monthausser discovers a plot to establish an international dictatorship of agencies.

All names in this book are purely fictional. The author has no evidence that the CIA or any other agency stages terror plots or manufactures evidence.

Prologue

Most people who knew David Monthausser were surprised when they learned that he was close to retirement age. His dark full hair, muscular build, and boyish smile fooled most people into thinking he could not possibly be older than forty or at worst forty-five. Yet the calm behind his pale blue eyes was at least in part tiredness—tired of his job that had taken too many rapid turns lately, tired of spending too much time away from his family, and worst of all, tired of seeing things going to hell and not being able to do much about it. David had grown up with the firm belief that even though his country was to blame for a lot of evil in the world, he couldn't think of any other country that might have done a better job if given the opportunity. So if anybody had ever asked him, he probably would have said that he was a real patriot—he might have added the word "reluctant," but only for people who knew him well enough to see it as the facetious remark it was intended as.

It's not that his family was particularly tied to American traditions. Both his father's and his mother's families had fled Alsace just before Hitler invaded it. Both his grandfathers had fought in the First World War on the German side against the French. But each had his own reasons not to wait for the Germans to come back. His father's father had been active in the French socialist movement, and his mother's father came from a mixed Jewish-German-French family. So he knew he wouldn't be welcome in Hitler's world order. Both ended up settling in West Virginia to work in the local mining industry. David grew up speaking German, French, and a little bit of Yiddish around his extended family before he learned English in school. He found out pretty quickly that languages came naturally to him, and it was due in part to his ability to blend in almost anywhere that the CIA recruited him after he finished college.

When he met his wife, Elana, during his last year in college, her family had just fled from the Soviet Union. He desperately wanted to impress her, so he taught himself Russian with the help of an old textbook and a friend whose family was from

Minsk. The first time he came to dinner at her parents' house, he had brought flowers but was so nervous that he called them *knigy* (books) instead of *tsvety*. Her mother took it in stride and promised she would read them carefully. At the end of the dinner her father commented that he spoke such good English he must be working for the KGB. David didn't quite know what to say so Elana's mother jumped in to explain that in the Soviet Union only few people bothered to learn any foreign languages and most of them ended up working for the KGB.

After finishing college, David took a job at the CIA and was looking forward to what he thought would be a life of excitement around foreign postings and clandestine operations. Elana was far less thrilled having just left the Soviet Union behind; she was in no mood to go anywhere near the Cold War confrontations of the time. David spent the beginning of his career posted in Germany and France, watching over operations from a distance and mostly helping field agents with paperwork and guidance. Once the Cold War ended, David asked for a posting in the Middle East, sensing that the next big challenge would come from there. His manager told him to relax and enjoy the victory party like everybody else. But instead, David started fishing for contacts in Turkey and Lebanon and developed a network of contacts in the region. After September 11, 2001, everybody started asking why they had no network of Arab-speaking field agents. By this time, David had moved into the signal intelligence group working for Henry Fletcher, who had noticed his many talents and thought he was in the wrong place as a field agent.

SOMETIME IN 2004. MEETING ROOM IN LANGLEY.

Technically, David Monthausser's job was to lead a team in the signal intelligence department that was able to break into pretty much any computer in the world as long as a connection could be established. His second assignment was to crunch through enormous amounts of data provided by the CIA's cousins at the NSA and look for clues and patterns that would be invisible to normal people. None of these had anything to do with the reason why he was in the room today.

Henry Fletcher relied on David to get a read on strategic issues and to observe what other spy agencies were doing. He knew David was the best person to distill patterns from small bits of information and strategies from seemingly unrelated patterns. The various conflicts in the northern Caucasus region had left them all struggling to understand the FSB's response. The FSB was the successor agency to the KGB, and to the public it seemed like it was caught completely off guard by the violent attacks that had shattered Russia recently, which did not make a lot of sense given its tight grip of every aspect of life in Russia. Henry had asked David to take a close look at what was going on and to present his findings.

As he was closing his presentation, David summarized, "...as you can see from all these details, it is highly unlikely that the attacks we have seen lately were perpetrated by the militant groups they have been attributed to. My read on the situation is that the FSB has been running the show from start to finish. They used their own explosives, stolen from an army outpost that the Chechens or Dagestanis would have a hard time getting access to. They blew up apartment buildings and train stations with complete disregard for human life in order to swing public opinion in favor of a previously highly unpopular attempt to keep these breakaway regions in the Russian Federation and to resort to a violent crackdown in those regions. As far as we can see, this was highly successful and amounts to what I call an 'Anderssen Gambit' in reference to a nineteenth-century German chess player who was famous for sacrificing important pieces in return for a positional advantage and often a quick checkmate. It is a highly risky strategy both in chess and in real life. But I think we need to be aware of it being used so that we can defend against it. Any questions?"

"Yes. I can see why we'd have to know about this to defend against, but wouldn't it also be a highly useful offensive strategy?" David had expected this type of question from Ron Polanyi. He had called him Ron the Hun in private conversations before, and the nickname had spread like wildfire around the agency.

Ron was the stereotype of a square-jawed military man with a mind that tended to separate the world cleanly into friend and enemy—the latter had to be destroyed, the former saved from the latter. For Ron, there was no middle ground and no room for other games to be played. His single-minded pursuit of the "us-against-them" philosophy made him the go-to person for the neoconservatives after 9/11.

"I am hoping that you are not seriously suggesting we should kill people to swing public opinion in a preferred direction, or are you?"

"Not at all. But I'm wondering why the FSB, if it was really running the show start to finish as you say, wouldn't simply expose the threat rather than blowing up the bomb. They could take the credit, look like heroes, and still point to a very real problem that requires fixing."

"Likely because they felt it would not have had the same impact."

"Right, but since the American public is far more sensitive to perceived terrorist threats than the Russians are, we could use this more moderate strategy for ourselves, right?"

"I don't think this would be ethically appropriate."

"Just think of the implications this could have on agency funding, political support, even simple things like running projects under a false flag. David, you're a genius. This is great!"

Assistant Director Victoria Felton jumped in to take the edge off the discussion. "We are not in a position to discuss operational strategy here, Ron. I have to agree with David. This would have enormously risky implications both through public exposure and the inevitable mistakes that will happen along the way. We should look at these patterns strictly under a defensive perspective."

Ron clearly was not happy with this outcome but chose to stay quiet for the moment.

David gave Henry the "didn't-I-tell-you" look as they were leaving the room.

An hour later, Ron was in Victoria's office. Victoria had made a quick career in the FBI and came into the CIA as a political appointee. When she arrived, the agency was rife with rumors about how she got the job. Her Barbie-looks and stylish outfits only added to the suspicion that there must be some truth to the gossip about her cozy relationships to "the executive floor at the DoD." In truth she was a capable manager and a skilled politician who knew how to navigate the cutthroat traditions of Washington.

"Victoria, you of all people should see the potential of this thing."

"I do. That's why I'm not going to let you touch it."

"You have to be kidding. Look at it this way: thanks to the NSA, we get the entire content of every e-mail ever written, and we can listen to every phone call ever made. All we have to do is filter out some of the conversations to find the occasional shifty character who is ready to commit a crime. We contact them, set them up with whatever they need, then we arrest them before they pull the trigger; the threat potential remains predictable, and we consistently show up as the heroes who save the day—how much better could it possibly get?"

"Classic entrapment. And you think this is ethical?"

"Who the fuck cares? All I'm talking about is picking out some people who sooner or later would have committed one of these crimes anyway. All we do is fast-track them and catch them before it happens. Nobody suffers, everything is great."

"I don't think so. That's not what we are here for. I believe you still remember the trouble we got ourselves into when we manufactured evidence of weapons of mass destruction in Iraq, don't you? What you are suggesting is ten times worse."

Ron was well known in the agency for having gotten a boost in his career path when he was eager to fill the perceived needs of the so-called neocons who asked for evidence that Iraq was manufacturing weapons of mass destruction. This brought him to the attention of Director George Tenet, and suddenly he was entrusted with critical jobs and showed up in every strategy meeting.

Ron walked out of Victoria's office rolling his eyes. But he knew exactly what he had to do.

Chapter 1

FOUR YEARS LATER. PURCELVILLE, VIRGINIA.

David had taken off early from work. Henry had said he should "get the hell out of here for once." He drove on the Harry Byrd Highway toward his house near the West Virginia border. After Nicole was born, he and Elana had settled just outside the suburban sprawl where they thought things were a little slower and quieter.

The early years were difficult because of his travel schedule, and it hadn't gotten much better recently since he was rarely home and his work schedule kept him chained to his desk most of the time.

He had just turned from Berlin Turnpike onto West Main and was still thinking about how his life seemed to be drifting rather than moving along the ambitious trajectory that he had once aimed for when he saw a group of teenagers and stopped his car.

"Gelato at LoCo with your old man?" he yelled across the street. "Bring your friends."

The exasperated look told him he still needed to work on finding the right tone for his teenage daughter. They sat down at the coffee shop.

"Your friends didn't want to join?"

"Dad!"

"Okay, I just thought..."

"You don't get it, do you?"

"What were you doing? Just hanging out?"

"Why do you care? What are you doing here anyway? It's not even midnight yet."

"Took off early, figured we'd make a nice dinner."

"Really?"

"No. I'm exhausted. I needed a break."

On their way home twenty minutes later they were stopped by a fire truck as they tried to turn into Sayre Court.

"What happened?"

"Bomb went off down the street."

"Which house?"

"Third on the right—the colonial."

He turned the car and sped off. He knew their lives had been turned upside down.

"What the hell are you doing? That was our house!"

"Exactly."

"So why are you driving away? What about Mom?"

"Standard procedure. I have to take you to the office. We will meet Mom there."

"What if she was in the house?"

"Police and fire department are already there. They know what to do."

"Are you insane? Stop the car. Let me out. I hate you!"

He dialed his assistant's line.

"Jenna, it's David. Henry still there?"

"One second."

"David—glad to hear you're okay."

"So you know?"

"Meet me at the deli on Georgetown Pike."

When they arrived in the parking lot, Henry didn't waste much time. "Leave the car, get in the van. We'll take you to a safe location." If he was surprised to see Nicole, he did not show it.

FREDERICK, MARYLAND. CIA SAFE HOUSE.

"Your daughter will have a new identity and be placed in an unrelated witness protection program. The federal marshal has been told that she witnessed a drug cartel assassination. You will stay at headquarters for a while until we have a location prepared for you. After that, you'll be transferred to a secure location with a new identity and will retire there with light supervision until we find out what the hell is going on. Any questions?"

"How can I communicate with my daughter?"

"You can't."

"What if I refuse?"

"Not an option."

"My daughter just lost her mother and you are separating us? Do you have any idea what you idiots are asking?"

"You barely have a relationship with her. She is finished with high school and was going to college anyway. We will place her in a good school, and once this mess is cleaned up, you can re-connect—or connect for the first time as it were."

David looked toward Henry, who had not said a word, then faced his retirement handler. "You bastard."

"David! With me." Out in the hallway, Henry did his best to smooth things over: "Yes, he's a rotten asshole—all retirement handlers are. Yes, it's not fair, but it's the best we can do. David, please!"

On the upside, all three of them had a beautiful funeral ser-vice at his wife's temple three days earlier after they all died tragically in a bomb explosion that blew through the gas line and started a raging fire. Even being the religious cynic he was, he had to admit it was a nice touch reading his own obituary and the very complimentary comments of his friends.

A few people in the fire department had to be briefed and given a stern lecture on national security. A local detective earned a promotion and a possible career path with the feds. And the medical examiner for Loudoun County had to be con-vinced to sign paperwork for three badly burned bodies even though the remains went straight to the feds.

David knew there was little he could do. This was an attack directly into the heart of the agency, and whoever was able to pull it off needed to believe that they had succeeded.

Chapter 2

FIVE YEARS LATER. OUTSIDE LA POBLA DE LILLET, CATALONIA.

Pablo had just come back from the market. He liked to walk into town and carry whatever he needed. It made him feel a connection with the way things were in older—healthier, he thought—times. Anybody taking a close look at his cottage high up in the mountains would likely have wondered about the amount of electronic equipment. But in his five years here, nobody ever visited.

Most of his days were filled trying to set up this old farmhouse as a fully self-sufficient mountain farm. He built a greenhouse, he had a decent sized garden, and electricity was generated by his solar cells on the roof and on the side of the hill. He only needed to go to the market to get meat and cheese. Other than that he never saw people.

This day was different. He had a sense as soon as he came around the last hairpin turn of the walkway. Not that he saw anything specific. But he checked the entrance more closely. He reviewed the alarm system immediately. He did not send an alarm to James, though, in part because he didn't really have anything to tell him—also because he couldn't stand the thought that somebody was watching him at all times, so the idea that there was stuff they didn't know about always tickled him. But he felt something was wrong.

Twenty minutes later, he heard a sound he had not heard in five years. His doorbell rang. He opened the door and did his best impersonation of a non-hospitable mountain troll with a grouchy "Si."

A sweaty thirty-five-year old mountain biker asked in heavily accented Spanish about Andorra. Eyeing his bushy blond eyebrows and broad shoulders, Pablo thought he looked like a bad impersonation of the young Robert Redford. And his Spanish was barely comprehensible.

"Vouz preferez Francais?" Would he rather speak French?

"Oui. Eh, peut-être Allemand?" German tourist, down here? A surprise indeed.

"Ja, ich kann Deutsch." He managed to put on a vaguely Spanish accent hoping this was a random tourist who could easily be fooled.

"I'm trying to get to a town called Soldeu in Andorra. How far away is that?"

"Already late. Too far for today."

"Oh my god. Any towns in that direction? Any place to stay?"

"Nothing. There is La Pobla in the other direction."

"I really need to be there tomorrow to meet up with my friends. Any chance I could stay here? I have my own food. I can sleep on the floor. I promise I will not be any trouble."

Either way this spelled major trouble. He could refuse, which was highly suspicious in this area where everybody went out of their way to be friendly to tourists, especially when they showed up on a bike. Or he could let the stranger in and get an earful from James in their next weekly session. Somehow the prospect of rattling James's cage a bit provided a promise of rare entertainment, so he opened the door and said, "Kommen Sie nur rein." Please come in.

He held out a hand. "Pablo Poixtras."

"Markus Bromberger."

"There is a couch that pulls out over there. You can put your bike in the shed or just leave it outside—nobody comes here; it will still be there in the morning."

Pablo made dinner using some of the pork loin he brought from the market with a porcini sauce and some leeks—both results of his sustainability plan to grow most of the things he needed. Same with the red wine that grew on the side of the hill and fermented in the basement.

Pablo stayed mostly quiet over dinner while Bromberger talked about his bike trip and the group he was trying to catch up with. After listening for a while to drawn-out vowels and shortened word endings, he asked, "You're from Nürnberg?"

"Neuendettelsau."

"Na, aah ned weid." Realizing he just disclosed a piece of his personal history, Pablo searched for a credible explanation while Bromberger asked the obvious question: "How come you speak Fränkisch?"

"I worked in Illesheim for a few years." He instantly cursed himself, realizing he had just given the location of a military installation, thus putting in question his identity as a Catalan mountain resident. Clearly his attention to detail wasn't what it used to be after a long break.

He decided he'd stay quiet now and listen to endless stories of biking exploits rather than risk another slip. In the middle of a story about yet another nasty climb up a mountain pass, Pablo froze stiff as he noticed the edge of papers sticking out of Bromberger's bike bag.

"How do you like the porcini mushrooms?"

"Absolutely delicious."

"Grown right outside, under the oaks over there. You passed them on the way up."

"Wow. I had no idea."

"Hard to notice since they grow mostly underground. Come, I'll show you." And he got up and opened the door before Bromberger had a chance to object.

On the way to the little group of oak trees, Pablo talked about his plan to grow all his food right on the fields outside. When they reached the first tree, he took the porcini knife from the bag he kept there and walked over to where he had harvested some of the mushrooms earlier to push aside some of the leaves and look for more. As Bromberger bent down to take a look, Pablo grabbed his arm, kicked his leg backward, threw him on the ground, and held the knife under his ear.

"Who the fuck are you and what do you want?" He demanded, dropping all pretense and switching to English.

"Look, like I told you—"

"Shut up. You were watching the path as I walked up. You did not travel the pass roads you were telling me about, and you speak Fränkisch with an American accent. And you have papers in your bag that have a filing code used by the CIA. Tell me one more time you're a tourist and you'll bleed out right here where nobody will find you in a long time."

"I was sent by a group of people who have taken an interest in your case."

"What the fuck?" The edge of the knife started pushing harder against the neck.

"Seriously. I can prove it. Let me just get the file."

"You can't. House is under constant surveillance. That's why we are out here—the only way you stay alive. This is your one chance: What is going on?"

"I am a courier. I work for a group of people who want you to have the files."

"What sort of people?"

"Rich and not happy with the way the country is going. They see themselves as sort of an independent oversight committee."

"Names."

"Sorry."

"Why?"

"They all want to live."

"No, I meant why bother. It's bad enough that politicians want to tell us what to do. Now we need a bunch of rich amateurs interfering on top of it?"

"Can you please get the damn knife away from my face? I came all this way to find you. I promise not to go anywhere."

Pablo relaxed the pressure somewhat but kept Bromberger pinned to the ground.

"Your case...your death...was used as justification for a huge expansion of the clandestine surveillance program—even hiding here in the mountains, you must have heard."

"So what? My house was bombed by a bunch of Koran-wielding nut cases. They killed my wife and had every intention to kill me and my daughter. Damn right we want to know what's going on, and if we have to listen in on a thousand innocent conversations before we filter out the one we are looking for, who cares?"

"We are not talking just thousands. The NSA records every single call made. The death of one person—or three if you believe the papers—is used to justify a continuous panic. Regular people are talking about the threat potential from terror attacks the same way they used to talk about nuclear fallout and mutual destruction back in the days of the Cold War. Every month, the papers have another story on some terrorist plot that has been intercepted."

"So?"

"So, we don't think there are any plots. It's part of a plan to justify continued supervision."

"And you know this, because..."

"Some of our members are directly in contact with the people on the inside of your agency."

"Look, I still don't see what your problem is. Why don't you let the feds do their jobs and keep the bad guys off the street?"

"We think this is used as a tool to undermine the very government that the agencies were set up to protect. Recently, a congressional hearing was set up to look into some topics related to the increase in surveillance. Two days later it was canceled due to pressure on the committee members. We know of at least one case where the pressure was coming straight from facts gathered in the congressman's private phone conversations."

"Then you expose them and that's the end—if you're right."

"Not that easy. This will be a long-term project."

"I still don't see what any of this has to do with me. Where I come from, liberty is not something we extend to people who are trying to kill us."

"You really think all of America tried to kill you?"

"You know exactly what I mean."

"I do. Problem is we always thought compromising some of our liberties was acceptable as long as we trade them for extended safety. As it turns out, the balance is very lopsided."

"And you think I'm part of that machine."

"You were. Now it looks more like you are one of the victims caught up in it. Your case came up while we were looking into how it all started. Some of our members were appalled by how this was handled and thought you should be told what is going on. Some even thought the fact that you are alive should have been made public immediately. The majority was against taking any action, but I'm acting on behalf of a minority opinion."

"So you decided to play with fire and use me as kindling. Thanks a lot."

"At least take a look."

Pablo thought about it for a while and said, "I'll look. But that's all I promise. One more question: What's with the Fränkisch act?"

"I'm from Michigan. My grandfather taught me the language as he grew up with it. I studied German in high school and college, and then worked in Germany for a while. A little of my grandfather's Fränkisch always stayed with me."

"Just so you know: nobody talks like you do anymore. But you'll have to keep it up while you're here—for the camera."

As they went back to the house, the conversation shifted back to farming topics, the problems of growing porcinis in relatively dry climates, and the advantages of growing red wine at high altitudes. Nothing that James could possibly object to, even if he were able to find a Fränkisch translator. It did dawn on Pablo that his visitor might have suspected the place was under surveillance and picked the language for that reason. Maybe he was a little smarter than Pablo was willing to give him credit for.

Next morning, Bromberger left the files in the oak forest next to the mushrooms. They arranged to meet a week later in La Closa, a bar in the little village of Castellar. Bromberger had a good point when Pablo tried to object to a second meeting: What was so urgent in his schedule?

For the past five years, most of Pablo's entertainment consisted of playing little pranks for James's benefit. In the first few months, he got himself into trouble for placing little "gifts" for James in front of the various video cameras. Some were just silly, others slightly obscene. He never got as much as an acknowledgment from James except in one case where he finally showed signs of severe irritation. Next morning, Pablo decided to show up with a peace offering—a clay statue carved with James's facial features in a Hulk pose, ready to scream. Unfortunately, James lacked any capacity for humor, and instead of a chuckle, he offered a visit from some equally humor-free HR lady in their next meeting.

Pablo knew James was in charge of monitoring multiple retired agents who lived under similar conditions—remote areas, need for isolation. James's job was to supervise and ensure there was no intrusion and that nobody got any ideas about bypassing the controls. After his pranks earned him nothing but trouble, Pablo decided to test James's attention. He knew James was one of the most obsessive-compulsive people in the universe, so he had to step lightly. He also knew all the rooms had video surveillance from more than one angle. And all communication was sent through a proxy server for filtering and monitoring.

Fortunately, he had always been pretty good at figuring out ways around such gates, or childproofing as he called them— this was one of the reasons he was reassigned to the SigInt group in 2002 after a long career as a field agent. His first step was to give James the occasional "maintenance window." He blamed it on the solar cells not providing reliable power. Some of the outages were real. In other cases, he triggered a short only to set up his own snooping system before he turned everything back on. Now he could see what James saw and start testing his loopholes. Eventually, he came up with a way to run a double-proxy that allowed him to create a dual stream for his IP packets—one for James, the other for himself. The video was a little trickier. He ended up capturing many hours of footage and splicing it in so many combinations that he could fill almost a week with random activity that would raise no immediate suspicion. The biggest challenge was to make sure he wouldn't show up on multiple cameras at the same time.

To the monitoring station, his feed looked just as boring as everybody else's. In reality, he was able to do all the things he was not supposed to. He figured out pretty quickly that his daughter's witness protection had sent her to Syracuse University where she was listed under the name of Erica van Wyden.

He watched her Facebook and Instagram accounts, read her Twitter feeds, and established a secret communication protocol with her by using an anonymous chat service. He was a bit nervous about this last part since he figured her outgoing connection might create a red flag with whoever monitored her. But he hoped they'd keep her on one of their longer leashes.

He also couldn't resist the urge to use his video-splicing skills to be absent for an entire day or sometimes even multiple days to go on bike rides through the mountains—yet another thing they had told him not to do. He had bought a touring bike and kept it under a tarp half a mile into the forest. He was pretty sure James would have no way of finding out as long as he remembered to change into his regular clothes before he reentered the video stream.

A WEEK LATER. CASTELLAR.

Pablo had been to Castellar only a few times. He usually got his supplies in La Pobla and generally stayed away from people as much as possible. This time, he had no choice. He still hoped Bromberger would simply not show up or the files in his backpack would turn out to be James's retaliatory joke on him. But he knew better. Not only did James lack capacity for humor, but his instinct told him Bromberger would be right.

Bromberger surprised him when he showed up. He didn't recognize him until he sat down at his table. Not bad for an amateur—or was there more to his act?

"I suppose you had a chance to read the material?"

"Yes. But I have a few questions first."

"Fair enough."

"How did you find out about me?"

Bromberger took a deep breath—clearly this was a long story. "Five years ago, your entire family was killed and buried in Leesburg cemetery. It was high-profile case and all over the news—a brazen attack by an al-Qaeda-associated group directly into the heart of the CIA. There was no doubt or uncertainty to the facts."

"Right, can't get a better cover if you want to vanish."

"Around the same time, two homeless people were hit by a car near Little Rock, Arkansas. The two, an older man with a teenage girl, were dead on the scene. The local police were planning to run their fingerprints through the system in hopes of finding any living relatives. But before they got around to it, the bodies were claimed by what the police thought was their family. Since the driver, a local construction worker, had been killed in the crash as well, there was no point in pursuing the topic.

"The chief of police assumed nobody had taken their fingerprints yet and simply closed the case. As it turned out, a young police officer had taken the prints but had not run them yet since he was out sick the next day. When he came back, the bodies were gone, the case closed. He asked his boss what to do and was told 'you can always get them framed—or just keep them in your desk.' Clearly there was no need for anything further. The officer kept the prints in his desk for the last five years.

"In the meantime, a woman from Florida filed a missing persons report for her seventeen-year-old daughter. She suspected her ex-husband had abducted her, but when the police checked his California home, they were told by the neighbors that he was working construction at an oil pipeline in Alaska. A phone call to the oil company confirmed the story, so the search went cold, and police kept looking for a seventeen-year-old girl.

"Three years later the construction worker who provided cover for the ex-husband was arrested on drug possession and police started connecting the dots. They thought the ex-husband was still at large and started a nationwide search. But it took another year before a certain police officer in Arkansas read about the case and got curious. He tried to run the old prints and his access was denied—redirected by a filter your friends had put in place earlier. He wasn't ready to give up and made some phone calls, which resulted in a visit at his home by people you probably know. He was told to keep his mouth shut or look for a new job. But he had already told a close friend.

"And that's how the report about this strange case ended up in a stack of cases the Missing Persons Help Center was looking into. One of our directors is a board member and was curious who would steal two dead bodies. She started looking for high-profile cases around the same time and yours was the leading candidate..."

"But I'm sure there were other cases."

"True. We had a number of candidates, but yours was always the most suspicious. Getting confirmation wasn't easy so we had to hack the CIA's archive."

"You did WHAT? Go back to where you came from. Goodbye." Pablo got up and started to walk away from the table intending to ask James for a conference call with Henry immediately.

"Sit down; relax. We had the best expert you could possibly get—same person who designed your system."

Pablo thought this through. He couldn't rule out that Mario had defected, but in that case his system would have been changed and probably replaced with traps to catch an intruder who was using his knowledge. And if he hadn't defected, this could be a sting operation to see whether he'd take the bait. Or Mario had started working as a double agent. He could not think of a single scenario that had any potential for an acceptable outcome.

Guessing what went through his head, Bromberger said, "It's not what you think. He is still working for the CIA. We approached him under false flag to do a vulnerability assessment."

"That may buy you a few weeks, but they will find out."

"Yes, but we hope to be past the point where it matters by then."

Time pressure. The death of any good plan.

"What makes you think you're not being watched while you snoop around the CIA? Do you see the two hunters at the bar? How do you know who they are? How about the waiter? Do you know who he works for?"

"The waiter has worked here for at least three weeks. I can't rule out that your agency has put him here long term or that they knew I was coming. But let's face it: they have all but forgotten you by now."

Pablo considered what Bromberger had said and it pained him to admit that he had a point.

"Okay, so you found me and you confirmed your suspicion. But it does not change anything. Nothing in the file you gave me is different from the story as I know it. A bunch of Islamic nuts tried to kill me and my family. We told the public they succeeded to throw them off track."

"Maybe. Except if that were the story, wouldn't we rather tell the public that they didn't succeed?"

"Unless we want them to celebrate while we come back to hit them."

"And where has that gotten us? Have you had any conversations with your boss? They would have needed your help, if anybody was investigating, wouldn't they? They'd need to figure out who to hit. They would want to do it publicly."

He had a point. Why did he never think of that? And what did it mean if the agency was not interested in looking into this case? An al-Qaeda group running around putting out hits on agency personnel and there is no retaliation? Not likely. What really bothered him were conversations with Henry he remembered about the need for expanded surveillance. Henry was very troubled by the idea that there might be US citizens who act as sleeper cells and suddenly pop up to act and start killing Americans. Henry's point was, "How do you know what all these people are thinking unless we check?" This was just a few weeks before the bomb.

"It took us more than ten years to find bin Laden." A lame attempt and he knew it.

"You had an al-Qaeda group infiltrated. Says so in your file. Wouldn't that be a good place to start looking? Did anybody do that?"

They did not. Erdal was his contact inside the cell, and he had insisted he would never talk to anybody but David—they would have needed his help. Nobody asked in five years. *Damn. How could I not have seen this?*

"So what do you think I should do?"

"Talk to your contact."

Five years ago, Erdal had infiltrated a small cell that was forming in the town of Erzurum in eastern Turkey. Most were Turkish nationals, not happy with the secular ways of their country. But the group also had one Yemeni and one Saudi member, both advocates of more direct attacks against the United States rather than focusing on creating an Islamic state in Turkey. The involvement of these two was the primary reason the CIA started to become interested.

There was no way Erdal was still in place. If the group was responsible for the attack, it would have to dissolve immediately afterward. They could have found out that he was an informant and killed him—this was the leading theory at the time about how they found out about David Monthausser's identity. Or he could have switched sides, in which case nobody would find him now.

"Erdal lives in Hyeres as an Algerian immigrant under the name of Mehdi Brahimi."

Pablo almost choked on a piece of cheese. "Are you serious?"

"We are reasonably sure. We have some friends at the DCRI who were worried about him. Not as a radical but as a potential CIA operative on their turf." DCRI was short for Direction Centrale du Renseignement Intérieur, and it was roughly the French version of the FBI.

He started wondering even more about the nature of Bromberger's group. If they had connections to multiple agencies, they were either extremely naïve or extremely dangerous. Neither would bode well for him.

"You're full of surprises. In my line of work, that's not a compliment."

"Look, you have no reason to trust me. But if you think you can trust your employer, you're dreaming."

"What do you want out of this? Why are you feeding me information?"

"We think secret agencies create a lot of injustice, and we'd like to help fix some of this."

"You mean you want to stir up trouble and accuse people? Trust me, lots of things are much better left in the dark."

"If you want to return to a normal life, we are your only option."

"Oh, really? I don't even know what a normal life is. Everything I ever did was based on deception. I have no idea how to do things differently."

"I know you're bitter. I'm sure I would be if I were in your shoes."

"You have no idea what my shoes feel like."

Bromberger was struggling for words. "You're right. I'm sorry. If you want to forget about the whole thing, I'll walk away and I promise you will not hear another word from any of us."

The thought was tempting. But his curiosity tempted Pablo even more. There was just one more thing he needed to know.

"One more question: I'm sure you have also checked on my wife?"

"We did after we confirmed what happened to you. We have no way to be sure. But if it had been a cover-up for three people, I think they would have looked for three bodies, not two. They probably would also have debriefed you together—just like they did with you and your daughter."

"My daughter happened to be there because I brought her. I think they would have preferred it differently."

"I don't know. But we have not been able to find any evidence that suggests she is not in the grave in Leesburg. I'm very sorry."

Henry had said Elana was killed in the explosion and that her body was burned beyond recognition. Would he use a bold lie after all those years they worked together? Then again, who was he kidding—this was what they did every day of their professional lives, wasn't it? But to what end? All they ever did had a purpose, and he could not think of anything that gave Henry a motive to mislead him. What would have happened if she came to the house the same way he did and drove away—

wouldn't she have come in to the agency? Where else could she have gone? All their friends were part of the same group. Was there any reason for her not to trust the agency? And where would she go instead? None of this made any sense.

He looked up and realized that he had almost forgotten about Bromberger.

"Must be tough to suddenly realize that the people you relied on for years have turned on you."

"We don't know that."

"Your face seems to disagree."

Asshole! But a very observant asshole, he had to admit.

"So where do we go from here?"

"I go back home. I will write up a report for the committee and will go on to the next job. You have some thinking to do. If I were in your situation, I'd probably want to verify why I was parked indefinitely while my story was used as an excuse to create a surveillance regime that Hitler and Stalin would envy us for."

"If that was the plan, why wouldn't they just kill me?"

"Who says they didn't try? How do you know who really set the bomb?"

"I mean right now."

"That's an interesting question and I don't have an answer."

Maybe I have one, Pablo thought. Erdal had been one of the best undercover agents he ever worked with. If they planned to activate him again, they'd need his help. Or maybe they were hoping that either one of them would reestablish contact. It would explain all the excessive surveillance on him.

"So you are simply extracting yourself and I'm on my own?"

"We are watching you. If you need help, and if we can provide it, we might do so. But don't count on it. Take this. Don't spend it."

"You're trying to pay your share of lunch? It wasn't that expensive." He looked suspiciously at the one-hundred euro note.

"Keep it in your wallet. Make sure you don't accidentally pay with it. It has a tiny antenna built in that connects whenever it finds a Wi-Fi signal and it sends a ping. Then it disconnects."

"I do hope you realize the irony. You are objecting to con-stant surveillance, but you just told me that in addition to my current twenty-four-hour supervision, you are now providing a second layer? Can I at least go take a piss without anybody watching?"

"Actually—"

"Please don't answer that."

"Actually, I promise, we will not be sending agents to watch you or keep cameras looking for you. But here is a phone num-ber, just in case you need it—I trust you'll memorize it and not keep any written records?"

Maybe this wasn't so bad after all.

NEXT MORNING.

Walking back from his meeting with Bromberger, he thought he'd have to carefully weigh his options. But when he woke up the next morning his mind was made up. There was no way he'd get involved, and he would simply walk away. He made himself a breakfast of two eggs, scrambled with some home-grown hot peppers and a handful of mushrooms. He counted all the reasons not to get involved. He had no way to verify that Bromberger was for real. Who the hell knew who he worked for? He'd risk his pension and his cushy arrangement—after all he still got paid and didn't even have to work. To find out any-thing meaningful, he would have to contact Erdal, which was seriously dangerous for both of them. Erdal—as close to a friend as he had ever known in any of the field agents he led over the years. Still, how did he even know that he had not been turned or gone rogue? What if he was the source of all this trouble? Only one way to find out. *No, no, and no.* Except by the time he was done with breakfast, it had become a *yes.*

His plan evolved very quickly. He knew he didn't have a lot of time because of the stupid stunt they had pulled hacking into the agency network. After about three weeks, Mario would start asking about the results of the vulnerability assessment and everybody would know there was a leak. Also, he needed to buy himself enough time to get to Hyeres undetected. He could not just rent a car or take the train. He'd show up as a red flag immediately. So it was either walk or bike. It had to be more than three hundred miles. Walking meant he'd have no chance to get back before his cover was blown. So his only choice was to go by bike.

Approaching Erdal would be a bit ticklish, since there was no telling which side he was on. Normally, he would have reserved a few days scouting out his daily routine and then approached him when he could be sure Erdal was alone. He didn't have the time, so he'd have to figure out something else.

But first his weekly videoconference with James was coming up. His least favorite part of the week.

"Ah, so you changed your shirt for me?"

Crap. He had forgotten to turn off the video loop in the morning, and James actually paid attention.

"Spilled Tabasco on it. Can't hold the bottle straight any-more at my age."

"Henry is here today."

"Morning, David."

"Nice surprise. What made you get up so early?"

"No reason—we have not talked in a while, and I just want-ed to check in."

Something was up. He had spoken with Henry exactly once since he arrived in his mountain hideout. Why now?

"Hey, before we start: the Tour de France is moving through the area here, and I figured I'd go watch it next week unless you think this would be problematic."

"You really should not." James was always predictable.

"After all this time," said Henry, "I think we can relax things a bit, don't you think, James?" Now, that was a surprise—Henry wasn't normally the one to relax protocol.

"Well, I'd miss next week's meeting, and of course if there is anything urgent on the agenda…"

"Urgent? Um, I wanted to go over security protocols," said James.

"James, we do this every week. I recite them in my sleep and sing them in the shower."

Henry settled the issue quickly: "Go watch your bike race and then let's reconnect in two weeks. I want to see how we can get you back in the game at least part time. I could use your help on some things."

So that was it. Interesting. Why now?

"We can't really do that—he is not supposed to be on any active assignments."

"He won't be. I just need his opinion. Relax, James—it's not like we are picking the Mossad's pockets."

Wow, Henry bringing out the artillery to shut up James. This is getting seriously interesting. Years ago, James was involved in an operation to hack the Mossad's network. It was never officially sanctioned, but a couple of agents fresh out of training were overly eager to get their hands dirty. The hack was quickly detected and led to serious diplomatic complications—spying on your closest friends needs to be undetectable. Ever since then, James and his team got to supervise simple stuff, mostly retired agents who needed to be kept on a leash.

"So this is something like my vacation before returning to work? I'm actually getting excited!"

"Can't call it that. But yes, I'd like to make use of your spare brain cells."

"Looking forward to it."

He wasn't looking forward to it at all. He did not like the sound of it. And it was creating timing issues. It would take him at least four days to get to Hyeres and the same amount to return, which left him only a few days to try to connect with Erdal. Even a slight delay would make this trip a one-way ticket. His initial plan was to use the Tour as his excuse for the upcoming week and then blow off James with a lame excuse the next week. But now he really had to be back. Better start packing.

Chapter 3

Pablo had bought a touring bike with luggage racks, twenty-seven gears, and all kinds of fancy equipment two years earlier when he decided that part of settling into his situation meant finding ways to temporarily break out of the routine. He kept it out of sight of the surveillance equipment in his mountain cabin and used it only for day trips except in rare cases—a trip to Perpignan once to watch a rugby game, watching FC Barcelona's season opener against Atletico Bilbao another. Nothing very risky, but had James found out, he would have had one of his temper tantrums. Each time he felt liberated afterward—almost as if he were a normal person doing fun stuff on a Saturday afternoon. The bike was the only way to do anything without the risk of detection. A car registration would have created a record. Train tickets did not require identification, but he did not want to risk showing his face on a railway station security camera. And traveling by bus was just too cumbersome in this area.

His plan was to get to Perpignan on the first day, Montpellier the second day, Marseille on the third, and Hyeres on the fourth day. He could eat along the road and stay at campgrounds or small inns that would not ask for an ID. He was pretty confident that nobody would notice his illicit travel. Yet he knew this feeling too well. Something important was missing. All these years without active field duty—he must have lost his attention to detail. So what was it? He couldn't dwell on his anxieties; if he wanted to be in Perpignan by evening, he'd better get on the road.

One final run through his checklist. The video was set to loop, and James would watch him go about his daily business, if he paid attention at all. A secure tunnel was set in his firewall so he could log in from anywhere. He had told his daughter that he'd be traveling and that he would be out of touch for the next two weeks. All the electronics were set to reboot to their current state in case of a power outage. In Perpignan he planned to stop at an Orange Telecom store to get a burner phone and a SIM card. He would do the same in Montpellier, and whenever he needed an Internet connection, he would switch back and forth between the phones to avoid leaving any patterns. He could not think of any scenario that would break his cover.

As he passed through town, he stopped at the grocery store to get supplies for the road. The owner was Jose Fernandez, a retired pro biker and the only person in town who occasionally exchanged a few words with him. Jose had commented on his bike right after he bought it, appreciating a nice "grand vélo," as he called it.

"En vacance, eh?" Whenever Jose wanted to tease him, he spoke French. *Vacation? Of course, the packed bike.*

"Yes, watching the Tour as it passes the Col de Pailheres."

"You better hurry then; the best campgrounds will be taken by tomorrow."

He was right, the real Tour fanatics would occupy the best viewing spots days before the peloton actually arrived. Time to move before he got into a conversation. Fortunately, the first part of his trip was in the general direction of Andorra and the mountain pass that would be one of the highlights of this year's Tour.

It only took an hour before he cursed his decision to go by bike and wished he had at least prepared for this exercise. The first part of the road leaving town was a very mellow climb. The road was leaning against the mountain that quickly turned nasty as it approached the Coll de la Creueta. With just under two thousand meters of altitude, it was not exactly a major pass road, but at his age, it was enough to knock the wind out of his chest. At least the mountain was to the east of the road and provided some shade in the morning hours. Still, the heat was becoming unbearable by the time he reached the height of the pass. He was really glad when he saw the Masella ski resort and knew that most of the road to Perpignan would now be downhill. The rest of the road would remain under the tree line and with enough shade to keep him reasonably cool. Passing the local Bank Santander he noticed the clock that said 11:35, and he realized he'd have to pick up the pace quite a bit if he wanted to keep his schedule. Age really was a bitch.

He reached the French border an hour later at Puigcerda. He was old enough to remember the Franco years when both sides nervously patrolled the border, especially up here in the mountains for fear of infiltration by the other side. The old checkpoint was still there, albeit abandoned and now useless—nobody in Europe had to show a passport these days to cross a border. One more minor pass road at Mont-Luis and the rest was downhill to the coast.

He had not planned to stay overnight in the city of Perpignan, instead hoping to make it to one of the villages farther north, but by the time he arrived, it was almost 8:00 p.m. He stopped at the first Orange Telecom store he saw and bought a cheap HTC phone and a prepaid SIM card. He saw a "Premiere Classe" hotel across the street—it looked anything but first class, which was precisely what he needed right now. If he walked in this late and made sure he mentioned that he'd be on the road before breakfast, they would not keep a record—he could go unnoticed and the owner would save the taxes—it was le Sud after all, and Paris was far.

As tempted as he was to just fall asleep, he needed food. He had seen a much nicer hotel up the road and figured they'd have a decent restaurant. There was a big sign by the road for "Le Restaurant." And the neighborhood did look like it might indeed be the only restaurant. He didn't mind; all he needed was food and to go to sleep quickly.

Of course, there was no such thing as eating quickly for dinner anywhere in France. The waiter insisted on recommending a long list of specials "de jour," and it was indeed reassuring to hear that the anchovies had come in by boat this morning, the rabbit had been shot this afternoon by the owner's son, and the goat cheese used for the salad came from an organic farm in the hills near the Spanish border. The restaurant was almost empty except for some locals and a young couple across the aisle who seemed like tourists.

He decided to trust the rabbit recommendation and took the "menu"—the French way of saying "we'll organize all the courses for you." He had his tomato soup—made from the tomatoes in the backyard if you could trust the waiter—with a glass of red wine from Banyul, a town only a few miles to the south. Getting back into his field agent routine was not as easy as he had thought. He had to force himself to eyeball everybody to see if they might carry weapons, and then he attempted to tune his ear to listen to some of the conversations. In one case he had to find an excuse to walk up to the bar so that he could confirm that the two middle-aged men at the bar were discussing a hunting trip into the countryside. *This is tiring; I should not be back in the game.* When his pâté de campagne arrived, he overheard some fragments coming from the tourist couple. Americans. Young lovers, quarreling about plans for life. *Why are people always doing this on vacation?*

His rabbit in white wine sauce with fresh green beans had just arrived when the conversation got more animated. *Trouble in paradise.* Apparently, the American couple had planned to get married while on vacation in France, but there was talk about having second thoughts. No friends or parents were invited, she had run away from home to come with him, and now he wasn't so sure. Pablo had to force himself to keep his attention on the other diners as the conversation got louder. Too often simple distractions like this were used as a way to capture an agent's attention while he should be focused on his surroundings.

While listening to "I can't just go back to my parents" and "weren't you the one who said?" and indulging on the flan for dessert, he decided he had overreacted; there was no danger of an operation going on. He was still working on dessert when the noise level picked up dramatically as the American couple started a full-blown fight and all the heads in the restaurant turned toward them. Some of the French customers started shaking their heads at such an uncivilized dinner behavior. Ultimately, the unwilling husband got up abruptly, threw his napkin on the chair, and stomped out of the restaurant. *Quite the exit.* The waiter showed up to ask whether everything was all right, and the girl just gave him an exasperated look. Now that she was leaning her back against the wall with her eyes closed,

Pablo thought he recognized her face, which caused him re-
newed anxiety. After a while he blamed it on her age—she had
to be just about his daughter's age. She even looked a little like
Nicole with her black ponytail, dense eyebrows, and the fierce
stare he always thought was only used for being mad at your
father. *How I wish my life had been different.*

He could not bear the thought that Nicole had just started
grad school and he could not be part of her life except for the
occasional covert chat session. He even missed her graduation
last year. She had suggested a small "virtual graduation party"
as she called it, simply talking for a while in one of their online
chat sessions. It had moved him to tears—he missed his family
terribly.

Pablo kept brooding about his lost opportunities until the
waiter reminded him with a quick "anything else?" that it was
time to go. As he looked around, the room was almost empty
and he realized he had been sitting there alone for a while. *Get
your act together. Time to go.*

Outside, she sat on a bench, head between her knees,
hands clasped behind her head. Despite his no-contact rule, he
couldn't just ignore her. *What if she were my daughter?*

"Are you all right?" *Next time, work a little harder on the
accent.*

"What does it look like?"

"Sorry. I couldn't help overhearing some of your conversation. Do you need any help?"

"What's wrong with you? Are you trying to invite me to your
room?"

He realized how stupid he sounded. "I wasn't sure if you
needed anything."

"Are you some fucking nut job? Get lost."

So he did. Despite the exhaustion from the first day of biking, he barely slept. He was tempted several times to call
Nicole. But then what? *How have you been all these years? And
don't say anything, people are listening.* No, calling really was
not an option. He'd have to tunnel back through his secure

network and use the anonymous rendezvous server for a chat. Tomorrow.

At six in the morning he woke up sore with aching joints and ready to go back to sleep for a few more hours. *Can't afford that.* He got dressed, put the luggage on his bike and realized as he got started that there is nothing like the promise of piercing pain on a second long day of sitting on a narrow hard saddle. As he passed Le Restaurant on his way north, he felt the urgent need for breakfast.

"You're up early." As he turned he saw the girl from last night sitting at one of the outside breakfast tables. "Join me for breakfast? I owe you an apology."

"You don't. You were upset, and I was bugging you. Totally fine."

"I was making assumptions about you."

"Correct assumptions for most men. Swatting them away is the better option, trust me on that."

He expected her to at least smile at that comment, but her face darkened. "You're right."

"I didn't mean it to sound so pessimistic—I thought it was a joke."

No answer.

"So what's your plan? Going back home?"

"I haven't really thought ahead yet. My boyfriend—ex-boyfriend, I guess—was already gone by the time I got to the room last night. No clue where he went. This is the middle of nowhere after all. As for me, maybe I'll just hang around France for a while. Not such a bad place from what I'm hearing."

"You could go farther south to Barcelona—it's a great city, with much more to see than here in Perpignan. Plus, there is the bike race moving through in a few days—that's always fun to watch."

At this, she finally perked up. "Is it Tour de France time yet? I completely forgot! I used to race in amateur races. Did I see you pull up on a bike outside? You're not one of those scouts, or are you?"

"I wish. No, I'm just a tourist biker. I carry all my luggage and go from place to place."

"You have an accent I can't really place—are you from around here?"

"South of the border. Catalonia."

"Hah. Barely noticeable. You could probably pass as an American, as long as you don't tell anybody which state you're from. Have you lived in the States?"

Quick. What's your excuse? "Fifteen years at Merrill Lynch in New York. Worst job I ever had." *Please don't ask about mutual funds or stock tips.*

"A banker? I would have never guessed."

"Software. I built some of their networks used for the transactions." *Much better—back in my comfort zone.*

"So what are you doing here now?"

"Back to where I came from. I have a little place in the mountains, grow my own wine, some vegetables, just try to be independent as much as I can. No more banks."

"So what's your next stop?"

"Pardon?"

"On your bike ride. Where are you going?"

"Montpellier. About 150 kilometers north of here."

"Ah. The opera in Montpellier is on my list of things to see while we are here—while *I* am here," she corrected herself.

"The Opéra Comédie? Not in session in the summer, I think. But you can always see the building—it's great architecture."

"You'll stay in Montpellier or are you going farther?"

He thought about it briefly and decided there was no harm telling her some of his plans. "Going up the coast to Marseille and then to visit someone in a small town not far from there."

"Oh my god, I always wanted to ride a bike along the Côte d'Azur and go up into the mountains. Maybe I should get a bike and tag along with you. I'll drop you off wherever you are going and then continue by myself. What do you say?"

He was struggling how to say no, and his face must have been quite telling.

"Don't be *that* shocked. I do know how to handle a bike, you know. And I'm not that bad as a travel companion."

"What—you break up with your boyfriend one night, and next morning you're off to an extended bike trip with a complete stranger? Who for all you know could be a serial killer hiding out here in the hills."

"Banker, not serial killer. Close enough, but legally I think you're not considered armed and dangerous. Public opinion might beg to differ though."

She's actually serious. What now? "Believe it or not, I'm actually in a bit of a hurry. I have to be in a town called Hyeres in three days from now. You don't even have any gear and your luggage is probably in a suitcase." *Lame excuse but it should keep her from going any farther.*

"Backpack, not suitcase. And there's a bike shop down the road. I have enough money to buy a bike—shouldn't take more than an hour. C'mon, what's the harm? Just humor me—if I can't keep up, you'll just drop me and you're no worse off. And who knows, I might even be able to provide a little bit of slipstream for you."

"This is not like a bike race—once you have luggage on your bike, it works very differently."

"Please."

"I don't think you're rational after your fight last night. Honestly, I think you should go back to your parents."

"What are you, trying to be my father now? I'm twenty-three years old. I can handle myself. Tell you what—get on your way. I will definitely get myself a bike and maybe I will catch up with you before you get to Montpellier, or maybe not. I don't need my parents, and I don't need a substitute father either."

She was red in the face and he realized he had overstepped a line. "I guess it was my turn to make assumptions. I'm sorry."

She just glared at him across the rim of her café au lait.

"You know what—finish your coffee and let's go get you a bike." *What the hell am I doing?*

She stretched out a hand. "Thank you. By the way, my name is Lara."

"Pablo. Pablo Poixtras."

"I think this will be great!" Her smile was back now.

Once again, her face seemed familiar. While she was getting her luggage, he was wondering whether he had just made a giant mistake. It was still time to get up and just ride off without her. Except he had just disclosed his travel plans. Could this be some sort of setup? Only if someone was able to read his mind. He had not told a single person about his plans. Even Bromberger didn't know when he was leaving and how he would travel. And he was reasonably sure that Henry and James did not know where he was. Either way, he figured now that she knew where he was going, he'd be better off keeping her close. *Who knows, maybe I'll even enjoy the company.*

The bike shop she had seen did indeed carry a few travel bikes amid all the mountain bikes and road bikes. When Pablo spoke to the shop owner, he asked for a "vélo de travail" and realized immediately that he had made one of the classic mistakes of the English speaker. The shopkeeper was amused and corrected him, saying he was sure the bike would do just great at work, but they also had some very good travel bikes. He was hoping his new companion had not picked up on the nuance, and he just mumbled that yes, he was interested in traveling, not working.

"So we have the frame, wheels, luggage racks for front and back, the Shimano Ultegra equipment, a set of bags. Do you need anything else?"

"Just two extra sets of tubes," said Lara in French. "I hate fixing tires." She actually spoke decent French.

"Anything else?"

"Non, merci," she answered. "Actuellement...Could you keep my backpack for two or three weeks once I'm done repacking?"

The shopkeeper raised his shoulders in a gesture meaning "what am I going to do with it?" He agreed, though, when Pablo returned a similar gesture for "why not just humor her?" With that they were ready for the road.

"What will you do with the bike when you're done and ready to return?" Pablo asked.

"Who knows? Maybe I like it here and will stay."

She was right about one thing—she biked like a maniac and would have definitely caught up with him before Montpellier even with an hour head start. He would have looked pretty stupid had he tried a breakaway after breakfast. Plus, being able to ride in a slipstream was somewhat of a relief, especially with the nasty afternoon wind blowing inland from the Mediterranean. They had lunch in Valras, a little beach town full of Parisian tourists, and made good time toward Montpellier, passing Frontignan in midafternoon. They were going through the first suburbs around 4:00 p.m. after getting soaked in a surprise afternoon thunderstorm.

They had just turned into the Place de la Comédie and he was looking for a phone shop to get his second prepaid phone when she asked a question he had not considered yet: "So where did you plan on staying?"

"Ummh, I have a tent and was planning to pitch it somewhere near the beach."

Her face clearly said "not the camping type."

"I hadn't really thought about it when I picked up a travel companion."

She looked a little uncertain and said, "You know, I do have a travel budget—what if I pay for a hotel?"

This was getting seriously complicated. He couldn't just tell her that he could not use his passport for fear of the CIA being on his tail.

"Or are you on the run from the police and can't register at a hotel?"

"That's not it. But I had no plans to stay in a hotel and my passport is in my briefcase in my desk drawer in a small town near Barcelona. Nobody checks your passport inside Europe anymore unless you're staying in a hotel."

"That's okay. Remember I needed a passport to get here. We can use mine to register."

"Single room then?"

"Don't get any ideas, serial killer. You're on the couch."

"At least I've got my indictment downgraded from banker. One more day under suspicion and I might become a re-spectable citizen."

They found a room at the Oceania just off the Place de la Comédie and registered as "Lara Baincroft." As they approached the ancient building, Pablo looked around for security cameras and noticed none on the outside and only one camera guarding the elevator in the lobby. *Vive le Sud; nobody is suspicious here.*

"Are you nervous about something?"

"Me? Why?"

"You keep looking over your shoulder. I thought you might have friends here and didn't want to be seen with me."

"No, I'm just interested in these old buildings. Southern France is one of the few areas in Europe that hasn't seen any of the big wars, so a lot of the buildings are still in the original shape."

The parking attendants offered to store the bikes and saw nothing strange in people traveling with luggage on a bike and staying at a place like the Oceania. Pablo managed to evade the elevator camera with the help of his bike helmet. On the way to dinner he figured he'd suggest the old staircase, which was af-ter many renovations still the original one designed by the art deco architect Thomas Piétri in 1898.

"Lucky you, they gave us two single beds—no need to stay on the couch."

He was indeed glad. Two days of biking without preparation had taken their toll on his aging bones. "I'll need to run out real quick and find a phone store. Do you want to come and go straight to dinner after that?"

"Can we check out the city first? I've never been here."

Right, tourist—forgot. "Sure, we are right off the Place de la Comédie—all the good stuff is right around the corner."

They decided on a small restaurant called La Passe Compose in an ancient little alley where the facade whispered, "I'm at least five hundred years old," but the inside was screaming with neon colors and lights coming from under the bar. The only thing ancient appeared to be the wine list. Pablo would have expected a young hip crowd but was pleasantly surprised to see mostly people his own age. Montpellier certainly had changed since the time he was stationed here in the eighties.

"So how much did I hold you back on the first day?"

"I have to admit, having someone else break the wind occasionally wasn't the worst."

"Thanks."

"Sorry for being such a grouch this morning."

"That's all right. So how come you gave up New York for the Spanish hills?"

"Catalonian hills," he corrected her. "New York would have been all right. Working for investment banks sucks, though. How about you? What's your story?"

"I finished college last year and couldn't quite figure out what I wanted to do. Some friends tried to convince me to go to grad school. I did some internships. Then I met Jeff. He was getting serious very quickly, wanted to get married. My father didn't like him—pretty much the same story with every boyfriend so far. We decided to travel to Europe, get married here. And then he turned out a complete jerk. I have no idea what got into him. So there you have it. Story of my life."

"So maybe your father wasn't totally wrong about Jeff?"

"Jeeze. You and my dad would get along just fine."

"You have to admit..."

"He's an artist. His mood is different every day. My dad thought I should follow a more traditional pattern, solid day job, boring things to do on the weekend, that kind of thing. Jeff set off every alarm bell he knows."

"So you decided to not even look for him or wait for him where he left you? Seems a little odd."

"You heard him last night."

"Hard to avoid, yes."

"I don't need that kind of shit. I have some money in the bank. I will just travel for a while, and maybe I will come to a decision on what to do with my life all by myself. If not, I can still go to grad school."

"Have you called your parents and told them where you are? Or are they going to send the police looking for you?"

"What is it with you and that whole parenting thing?"

It took him a little while before he was ready to answer. "I have a daughter your age. When I don't know what she's up to, I'm worried sick."

"And you know what she's doing right now?"

"Um, no."

"Who is she dating? What kind of music does she like? What do her friends say about you? What did she do last weekend?"

He looked stunned. *How quickly can I change the subject?*

"I get it. Not that pretty either, is it?"

"No. It isn't."

The waiter rescued Pablo when he brought the foie gras ravioli and pointed out how it comes from duck liver with no force-feeding necessary to produce it.

"So where are you planning on going after Marseille?"

"Haven't really thought about it much yet. I always loved watching the Tour when I still raced. I could never figure out why the Ventoux is supposed to be such a tough mountain."

"Oh, just wait until you are at the bottom looking up. It's a giant rock blocking your path at the edge of the Rhone Valley. Getting up there with luggage on your bike is a real pain in the rear."

"You've been there?"

"Once. Many years ago."

"Wanna come?"

"I can't. I'm going to Hyeres, then back. And I need to be back before the eighteenth."

"So take the train. Barcelona, right? Shouldn't be so hard to get to."

"I might have to do that anyway. I'm not sure how long everything will take in Hyeres."

"Why is that? Your friends don't know you're coming?"

"Actually, they don't. I will have to track them down first. It's somewhat of a long story."

"Mysterious, aren't we?"

He started to curse himself for not having thought through a proper cover story. Then again, he hadn't expected to need one. Good thing she was not used to looking for suspicious signals. Anybody in his line of work or even just plain curious people would unravel his thin cover immediately. Lara seemed combative but not that interested in grilling him on any details. Still, he decided to steer the conversation into safer areas.

"Which fields were you looking into for grad school?"

"Forensic science."

He almost choked.

"I'd love to work for one of the government agencies. Even though they are getting a bad reputation these days."

"Are you sure about that? From what I'm hearing, the hours suck, the pay stinks, and your reputation among most of your friends will be ruined."

"You're reading too many crime novels."

"So what's the upside?"

"Doing something that matters. That helps someone somewhere. Not getting stuck working for a bank."

"Ouch."

As they got back to the hotel, Pablo noticed that there was a business center on the first floor.

"I'll need to go check on a few things real quick. Why don't you go up, unless you want to have a drink at the bar."

"I'll be upstairs. I guess you don't need me to wait up?"

"Not for me."

He found one of the workstations, googled "Lara Baincroft," and found barely anything. A few search results for bicycle races and nothing else. *Is she the only person left without a Facebook page?* He decided not to dwell on it and instead check on Nicole's elaborate status messages on Facebook, Twitter, and

Instagram. He looked through some of her pictures with friends, read her status updates about her weekend hiking in the mountains, read her blog post about a college privacy issue he barely understood, and then turned to her older pictures. As he looked at the graduation photo on her Facebook page, he suddenly felt cold sweat running down his spine. Right there in the picture was his travel companion Lara Baincroft standing about fifteen feet away from Nicole—or "Erica van Wyden" as Facebook had it. Except when he rolled his mouse over Lara's head, it read "Sara Baur."

Unless the two were twins, there could be little doubt. He checked Sara Baur's Facebook page and found nothing remarkable: exactly Nicole's age, went to Syracuse University with her, and according to her Facebook status was "in a relationship" with some art student called Jeffrey Oldermayr.

His mind was racing. What were the odds of one out of 300 million Americans being a classmate of his daughter? Intersect that with the odds of this person running into him out of 450 million European residents, right here in the south of France. He was a little rusty in his statistics, but he was pretty sure this was about as close to zero as you could get.

So he was set up. But how? How on earth was this possible? Piece by piece his analytical capabilities came back. He quickly ruled out the CIA. They would have never sent the same agent after him who was assigned to be his daughter's sidekick. He never doubted that there would be somebody at Syracuse who was paid by the agency to check in on Nicole. But it was much too dangerous to send the same person to meet up with him.

So if not the CIA, then who? He had a hard time thinking of any reason for a competing agency to have an interest. Everything he knew seemed to say he was sidelined for purely an internal reason and nothing to do with the Russians, Chinese, or any other agency. And even if he was wrong, they all would have taken the same precautions and used two separate agents since they'd know about the connection. Or was it possible that someone did not know that there was a connection and therefore sent the same agent? *Very low probability*.

Or could it be Bromberger's crew? He had said they'd never send agents after him. But it would be just about right for how much of an amateur enterprise the whole thing seemed to be. In this case, he'd have to split immediately. Somehow this seemed wrong, though—if she were part of Bromberger's team, she could have approached him openly rather than coming up with this convoluted story of hers.

He could not come up with any other party that might be interested and decided it would be best to simply watch for a while.

After getting past his panic and being upset with himself for getting tripped up that easily, he decided that whoever was behind this had to be primarily interested in Erdal. So after passing through Marseille, she would very likely not turn north toward the Mont Ventoux but insist on going to Hyeres with him. He would keep things quiet until they passed Marseille and then decide how to confront her.

He double-checked to make sure the browser was set to "private browsing," killed the session, and started a terminal to connect to his network and see whether any alerts had been set up or whether anything else had happened that could have made James suspicious. Everything was quiet.

When he came up to their hotel room, the light was off and she seemed asleep. Despite his exhaustion, he was not able to sleep for a quite some time.

Next morning he woke up to find out that Lara was already gone. He went down the stairs and found her at breakfast.

"So, ready for Marseille today?" he asked.

"Yes, I already checked it on the map—160 kilometers, mostly flat?"

"All along the coast, yes. We can either go through the wetlands of the Camargue or go a little farther north through Arles. If you're serious about going up the Ventoux, Arles gets you closer to it."

"I'm not sure whether I'm ready to climb yet. I am quite sore from yesterday and that was all flat. Maybe I should trace the coastline toward Nice and then get to the mountains."

And there we go; she's preparing to come to Hyeres. Aloud he said, "Probably the smarter choice. You can warm up by staying a little north of the coast and go through the foothills."

Chapter 4

SANARY-SUR-MER, EAST OF MARSEILLE.

They had left Marseille early and found a lunch place off the tourist beaches in a town not far from Toulon. Pablo was looking for a quiet place and found it in Sanary—a little restaurant called Pitchouline right on the main road that had a garden with some tables in the back. He was trying to avoid the high-traffic tourist areas like the ones they had just passed in Bandol to have the conversation he was dreading.

The owner of Pitchouline noticed their biking clothes and was interested in their travel plans and where they had been. They left it at being accidental travel companions and having independent plans.

"Seems like we will hit Hyeres pretty early. Do you plan to go farther this afternoon?"

"I figured we could have one more evening together before we split—as long as you don't mind my company?" She had actually made a pass at him in Marseille and he made it clear that he wasn't interested, which led to a somewhat amusing discussion about generational differences.

"I have to ask you a serious question."

"So ask."

"How do you know Erica van Wyden?"

She was a lousy actress. If she wanted to have a career with whatever agency she was with, she really needed to work on controlling her emotions, thought Pablo. She had panic written all over her face, her chin was trembling, and she had to squeeze her hands to keep them from flying off the table.

Pablo kept staring right into her eyes and did not say another word.

"We went to Syracuse together. But I suspect you already know that."

Nothing more than a nod.

"How did you find out?"

"Did you think I was stupid?"

"So you probably know that my real name is not Lara Baincroft. That the scene with Jeff was staged for your benefit and that I know who you really are."

"I guessed the former, suspected the latter."

"I was assigned to shadow your daughter and see if I could find any hints about your whereabouts."

"Whoa, slow down. Remember, I'm dead. My daughter is dead. How did you know we were not?"

"Honestly, I have no clue. I was told one day that the daughter of a high-profile CIA agent who had died in a fiery explosion had resurfaced and there were suspicions that something wasn't kosher. Since I was the only one who could be made to appear young enough, I transferred to Syracuse on a falsified student record. I tried to be friendly with her, but couldn't get very far—she's even tougher than you are. Plus, we had to be careful since we figured there had to be another shadow agent who was sponsored by your agency.

"Then a few weeks ago, we got lucky and received information from somewhere that you were hiding in the Pyrenees. The same source indicated that you were likely to travel to Hyeres, which threw us into panic mode. We are interested in the same asset as you because of the past history."

Great, so Bromberger has a leak. "Who is the 'we' in this?"

"I work for an organization that is loosely affiliated with Israeli security."

"Bullshit. The Mossad would never assign such a junior agent to a case like this, especially when it involves spying on an American agency."

"I didn't say Mossad. And I'm not the kid I've been posing as. We didn't have much choice. Normally we would never put the same agent on this job who shadowed your daughter. But we figured there is a pretty good chance that you didn't see me anywhere with your daughter—as far as I know there is only a single photo from our graduation that we weren't able to suppress. So we thought the risk was minimal."

"Why the interest in me?"

"We have some common history, even if you didn't notice us at the time. The agent who infiltrated the Islamic cell in Turkey for you—I believe you know him as Erdal—showed up on our radar early. We had our own operative in the cell, and we had suspected Erdal of being the ringleader until we found out he was working for you."

"We are talking about the same al-Qaeda cell that blew up my house and killed my wife?"

"Actually, they didn't. Everything looks like they were set up as the scapegoats. But we still don't know by who. We are pretty sure that whoever did this wanted you dead and was ready to accept the death of your family as collateral damage. After the explosion, Erdal left the group and disappeared. The remaining members figured they had been compromised and disbanded. As far as we know, they suspect Erdal to be the one who set them up. One of them is fighting in the war in Syria at the moment, another is on the Hamas payroll, and a third one is back in Yemen with a group that we are trying to infiltrate. The rest were minor players, and we have little interest in them.

"So at first we didn't really care that much about the whole incident. Just one more of the many mistakes of the CIA blaming the wrong group for a terror attack. Sometimes it looks like you guys can't even get the names of your adversaries straight. But then we found out that the Russians also had an operative in the group, as did the British. And once you were done counting all the major players, al-Qaeda was the only one left without representation. By itself that's not something that would have worried us yet. But then we noticed a pattern: this was the first case where the Americans blamed a group for something and the Russians acted as the source for independent confirmation. Later we found many more. And each time, we saw the same informants involved in the group. Except that Erdal had vanished and you were dead—or so we thought."

Now she had his full attention. This complemented Bromberger's stories perfectly.

"We were getting worried about what we heard from our own operative who insisted everybody else had to be wrong.

And you know how it works in agencies—you start trusting the misinformation of the other side more than your own people after a while. So finding your daughter in our facial recognition system a few years ago was a major breakthrough. Now we knew somebody was covering up. But we still didn't know who and what. And I'm hoping you can fill in some blanks."

"I still don't understand why you are interested in this to begin with. The group is clearly defunct, and all that's left is some internal CIA cleanup."

"I don't have enough insight, but I think the suspicion is there might be more to it, and we were hoping you could help."

"I wish I could. Honestly. I've been told about similar suspicions by someone who is not connected to the agency, and I'm trying to find an old friend to see what he knows."

"Erdal."

"Yes."

"So he is in Hyeres."

"I have reason to believe he is."

"Let's go talk to him then."

"There is no 'we' in this. If he sees me show up with you, he'll run. And any credibility I might have left with him will be shot."

"So what's your plan?"

"I go. You book us a nice hotel and wait."

"I need to bring him in."

"And I need to turn around and go back to Barcelona right now."

They both stared at each other for a while until he stretched out his hand and said, "Maybe we start over. David Monthausser—pleased to meet you."

"Nora Weizmann."

"Look, Nora, I'm willing to take a huge risk here operating without agency approval. You have a few choices. You can blackmail me by threatening to rat me out to the CIA. Problem is I would have no incentive to cooperate with you, and I'm much better off turning back and disclosing everything I know to my boss, which would get you into more trouble than me.

You can also try to follow me when I meet with Erdal. Keep in mind, though, that I was a field agent for twenty years, and I will notice your people. Or you can convince your people to stand down and wait for the results I bring back. I do promise I will share." *Even though it may depend on what I hear.*

She was quiet, chewing on her lower lip.

David asked: "One more question: What exactly are you doing here?"

"Isn't it obvious?"

"No. Everything I know is telling me this is an internal issue for my agency. I'm very surprised to hear that Israeli intelligence cares about this."

"All I know is we had agents in the same group. I'm supposed to figure out what happened."

"Five years later? With no activity since? You don't really believe that, do you?"

"No, but it's all I know."

"Then who knows? If we cooperate on this, we should both be clear on what our motivation is."

"I need to make a phone call."

"What? Right here in the middle of Tourist Central? I thought you guys were professionals? Is this amateur hour?"

"Relax. Not here. Did you see the boat rental place over at the harbor?"

"Yes."

"How are your sailing skills?"

"Zero."

"Too bad. But maybe you can at least hold the wheel straight while I work."

"You can get a secure connection in the French mobile phone system?"

"Yes."

"You're sure about that?"

"Yes."

"Okay, let's go."

They waited until they had sailed far enough outside the harbor area. Then Nora dialed a number on her phone, punched in a code, and waited for a call back. She left David at the wheel for a while with the instruction to simply hold it straight while she moved up to the bow to talk. After a few minutes she came back and said, "For you."

"Yes?"

"David Monthausser?"

"Yes."

"Pleasure to meet you. I have always admired your work—very subtle."

"Thank you. Who is this?"

"It does not matter. Nora tells me you have questions about our motivation."

"I do indeed. Why are you interested in CIA internal affairs?"

"That's not what it is. We think this might amount to an interagency conspiracy. One that we are not part of, but it does affect us. Hence, we need to understand it. We think you might have been caught up in it, which may align your interests with ours at least temporarily, possibly longer."

"You think I'm ready to defect."

"Mr. Monthausser, if I were to ask Henry Fletcher where to find you, would he say 'Hyeres'?"

"He would say I'm dead."

"Yes, but are you where Henry expects you to be?"

"Point taken."

"So let's assume we are on the same side for now. We are certainly willing to help, if we can. Nora tells me that you can establish contact with the person we are both interested in?"

"I believe I can as long as I will be left by myself."

"Very well. Can I ask a favor? I'd be grateful if I could spend some time with your contact in the near future. Would you ask him to cooperate?"

"I doubt that I have any leverage on this topic. Actually, once he knows I was able to find him, he might decide to vanish again."

"We might be able to help him with that, if that's what he wants. I assume the people he is trying to get away from are close friends of yours?"

David realized that he was about to break all ties with his former employer. This was getting quickly to a point where it was bound to blow up some way or another. "That's what I'm hoping to find out."

"You will keep in touch with Nora? I don't need to remind you that she has a habit of finding people, so there is no point in avoiding her?"

"So I noticed."

"Oh, and David: be careful. I don't have to tell you what you're messing with?"

"I am painfully aware of it."

"Au revoir and good luck."

"Thank you."

"Good talk?" Nora was smiling.

"Reasonable."

"Next stop Hyeres? Should we take the boat or the bikes?"

"I can't stand boats."

They checked into the Hotel du Soleil on the same afternoon and reserved a room for three days. If Nora was surprised that they were staying so long, she did not show it. He immediately set out to visit a secondhand clothing store to get a worn-out hoodie and ill-fitting jeans. He passed through a field on the way back and made sure he got enough dirt stains on both to prepare them for their purpose.

"Fashionable" was Nora's only comment after he changed into his new outfit, grabbed an empty Styrofoam coffee cup, and put some coins in it to become the neighborhood *clochard*.

He hesitated before taking his wallet, including Bromberger's one-hundred euro note, out of his pocket. No good would come from being traceable in the next few hours.

David made it to the neighborhood that Erdal was living in, according to Bromberger's information, just in time for people returning from work in the afternoon. He pulled the hoodie into

his face, held out his cup, and shook it occasionally to encour-
age people to add some coins to the existing ones. Few people
did, and they earned a polite "merci beaucoup, monsieur." It
was an immigrant neighborhood populated by Algerians, Moroc-
cans, and the occasional Senegalese. Very few women were in
the streets.

It was already dark when David was about to give up and
return to the hotel to try again next morning. He saw one more
person walking down the street and decided to wait for him to
pass. He kept shaking his cup asking for money, but this time
as this last person passed him, he grabbed his wrist and said,
"Monsieur, can you spare ten francs?" The grab to the wrist and
the curious use of the old currency term caused Erdal to look at
the face of the old beggar—only to freeze in shock.

"What is it? Can't stand looking at dead people? Come with
me and get out of the light."

"David. Mon Dieu!"

"Cut it with the French. I need to talk with you."

"I can't. Not now."

"Erdal, you can't run. You know I'll find you."

"You're good at what you do. But I'm already late. Meet me
here the day after tomorrow. Same time."

David didn't like it. Waiting two days was not good now that
his presence was known. If Erdal had gone rogue, this would
give him plenty of time to set up an ambush. Even if not, people might be watching them and decide they had seen enough
and would take them both in. "I don't think this can wait."

"Whatever it is, it has waited five years. It will still be here
when I see you in forty-eight hours."

David knew he had no way to force Erdal to come along, so
instead he said, "Okay, Thursday, 8:20 p.m., right here. I will
ask you for twenty francs. If you are not followed you tell me
that's crazy old money and keep walking. Three blocks farther
there is a narrow alley; we meet behind the trash cans."

"I know which one. If I say nothing, don't follow."

"I'm not new to this."

Erdal smiled—of course he knew that.

Nora didn't like the delay either and suggested simply abducting Erdal. She could get a team ready within forty-eight
hours. David assured her that there was no use in trying. They
could certainly snatch him, but they would not make him talk.
"Unless we snatch his family," she said, but once she saw
David's face she immediately apologized. *For now*, David
thought. *At least I know now what they are willing to do.*

"So what are we doing if he runs?"

"We have to take that risk. We have no choice."

"I wish we had eyes and ears on him."

He looked at her for a moment and said, "There might be a
way—at least for the ears. Do you have a Bluetooth headset?"

"Yes, why?"

"Let's pair it with this phone here." He took out one of his
burner phones. "How is your French? Can you pass as a
Parisian down here?"

"Probably not. Unless it's a very short discussion."

WEDNESDAY MORNING. RUE SAINT-FRANÇOIS, HYERES.

Yasemin was just about to leave the house to go to the
market—she liked to get her shopping done as soon as the kids
were off to school and Erdal had left the house. He had been a
bit strange last night asking her not to open the door for anybody and watch her back when she left the house. He had not
been talking like this ever since they had left Turkey. So when
she heard the doorbell, she checked from the living room window to see who it was.

A young woman looked right up at her. She said she was an
exchange student doing a survey for the political institute of
Grenoble University and just needed to show her a question-
naire.

"Thank you so much for talking to me. So many people
don't want to take the time."

"What is it about?"

"We are running a survey to find out how people feel about
the recent election gains of the Front National. I am a political

science student and am working on my doctoral thesis on the rise of parties on the radical right."

"About time someone took a closer look at these fools. Would you have a pen?"

Nora searched her pockets and said "Oh, I must have left it at my last stop."

As Yasemin went to the kitchen to find a pen, Nora turned David's burner phone on and stuffed it inside a sealed plastic bag into the soil of a nearby potted plant. She clipped the Bluetooth earpiece into the densely grown *Ficus* tree—she had it all done just when Yasemin came back.

"Here, let me just fill this out real quick, then I'll have to run out to the market."

"Thank you so much for doing this."

"You said you were an exchange student? Where are you from?"

"Vidin in Bulgaria."

"How nice." She was tempted to add that she was from Turkey, but even after five years, Erdal's warning to never talk about personal details were still top of her mind.

"Au revoir, madame."

"Au revoir."

Later that night she would tell her husband that an exchange student was asking questions about the Front National. He'd get agitated asking whether she left anything behind, where she was from, and how old she was. Her description of a Bulgarian in her early twenties who did not leave anything, did not touch anything in the house, and was a nice young kid calmed Erdal's anxieties.

Nora and David were taking turns listening to conversations in Erdal's house. After the kids were in bed, Erdal told Yasemin he'd have to meet an old friend the next day.

"Old friend? Same people we left behind in Turkey?"

"Not exactly. A real friend. But you're right—it's bad news. I thought he was dead. If he can find us, so can others. We need to be ready to leave."

"Who is this person?"

"Yasemin, please."

"Okay, what do you need me to do?"

"Keep essentials packed. Keep cash around. Do not talk to anybody. Even when they ask about the assholes of the FN. Please."

Later, a phone call. The sound muffled, probably not taken in the same room, possibly out on the balcony. David could only make out a few words, and he thought they might be in Russian, but he could not be sure.

"It sounds like your friend actually trusts you."

David felt rotten about listening in on Erdal's conversations. But he could not afford mistakes. "I don't like doing this."

"Better than getting killed because you miss something."

"I suppose. You're sure you want this for your career? You could still find a real job."

"Right, work for Merrill Lynch for fifteen years?"

"It would be less likely to kill you."

Thursday evening. Rue Saint-François.

The homeless man was back at 8:00 p.m. holding his Styrofoam cup and shaking it to solicit donations. When Erdal passed him, he asked for twenty francs and was told, "That's the crazy old money" with a shake of the head. *Street people get crazier every day.*

David let a few minutes pass and then followed Erdal to the alley.

"I'm sorry to put you on the spot like this."

"What happened to you?"

"Short story: bomb blew up my house, killed Elana, but missed me and Nicole. Agency declared us dead for the rest of the world and retired me in a mountain cottage. The agency thinks the group you had infiltrated pulled it off."

"They do? What do you think?"

"I think something smells foul. If the group had pulled it off, you'd either be dead or moving up in the hierarchy. Instead, you vanished. So something went wrong."

"Darn right it did. I remember it all clearly. Hani, the group leader, came to my house the morning after you were 'killed.' He told me a CIA agent had been killed at his house in northern Virginia and that his name was David Monthausser. He wanted to know if I knew you. He said we were blamed for the attack and as much as he'd love to take credit, he thought it was a setup.

"So I figured there are only two possible explanations. Someone else pulled this off and the CIA blamed us, which would raise the question why they'd be willing to burn me and it meant it was time for me to run. Or it was really done by our group and they did not want to tell me because they knew I was your contact, in which case it was probably too late to run.

"Yasemin and I left town the same afternoon, leaving every-thing behind. My parents have no idea what happened to me, and neither do hers. Our kids were young enough to think they belong here. But this does not make a lot of sense."

"Why?"

"If it had been our group, it would have been cause for cel-ebration. They would have taken credit. Same for any other group. The fact that you're alive could mean that someone wanted to burn your connections including me. But I don't un-derstand why."

"Me being alive is purely accidental. I was late coming home because I ran into my daughter on the way home."

"Who knew you'd be there?"

"Lots of people." *Really that many? He has a point.*

"If they wanted you dead then, why haven't they killed you since?"

"Possibly because they think I'm dead?"

"I think you've come to the same conclusion as I did: this was an inside job."

He had to admit that it was the only explanation that made any sense. "But not everybody inside knows I'm alive—actually most people don't."

"Anybody who goes through this amount of trouble would check very closely to make darn sure they succeeded. They'd also be connected to the very top. So why are you still alive?"

"I don't know."

"How did you find me?" A knot started forming in David's stomach. Was he really only alive to help track down Erdal?

"There is a group of people who are looking into CIA conspiracies. They found me and passed me some documents."

"And you believed that? David!"

He had to admit, it sounded much less convincing right now.

"Who knows where you are right now?"

"Nobody...except...the Israelis."

"What the hell happened to you—cat eat your brain? Why are you bringing the Mossad in?"

"They had an agent in your group and were already on your tail." He chose to leave out the part that they were really on *his* tail to get to Erdal.

"Who was it?"

"Don't know. They say he's active elsewhere now."

"So we are dealing with the Israelis helping a former CIA agent save his hide and embarrass the agency in the process. Do I have it right?"

"Not former, current."

"So former and delusional, great."

"Let's look at what we really know for a minute."

"That should be a quick exercise."

"Maybe not. We know that the agency needs me for *something*; otherwise I'd be dead. We also know someone was ready to kill me five years ago. So either something has changed or the current outcome was always planned."

"You think it's possible?"

"Not easily, but there might be ways to pull it off, yes. They certainly go through lots of effort and cost to keep me alive and hidden. What's strange is that they never asked me how to find you once they knew you had left Erzurum."

"Would you have known where to look?"

"No, but if I were in their shoes, I would have tried every angle."

"Any theory about why they didn't?"

"Only one: they knew I couldn't possibly know."

"How?"

"No clue. Unless there is a secondary source. One that would have told them that you cut ties or one that you are still in contact with—possibly without knowing."

"Yasemin is the only person I'm still in contact with."

"And we are reasonably certain she is not working for the agency, right?"

"David, I think I'd know—I've been married to her for almost fifteen years now."

"Okay. So then the next thing we know is that the agency has been expanding its covert surveillance program over the last five years. According to my source it now monitors all communications inside the US and a large percentage of communications in foreign countries."

"You believe these fairy tales?"

"At first I didn't. But then I read about a guy called Edward Snowdon who defected and started leaking NSA documents supporting the same theory. Now it makes sense. But to justify this effort, they need a constant threat potential and they need the occasional predictable success. This is not new. My boss was probing my thoughts on this just a few weeks before the attack on my house. He thought we should simply instigate our own attacks and defeat them so that we'd have a constant stream of good news while keeping people on edge about their safety."

"That's sick. Outright pathetic."

"Clearly you've never been inside an agency. I initially had the same reaction you have now. But I have no illusion about how the majority of agency personnel thinks on this topic." David thought back to a conversation he had with Henry Fletcher and Ron Polanyi and thought, *You have no idea how real this is on the inside*. He added, "The people who run this inside the agency actually call it a 'dictatorship of intelligence'— as if this wasn't an implicit oxymoron."

"But other agencies would see this for what it is and sooner or later the scheme falls apart."

"Not if you conspire with your fellow agencies around the world and make sure everybody's interests are aligned."

"Are you saying this is something the CIA cooked up with the FSB and the Chinese? You're completely crazy."

"I'm not sure how it came about, but we all know that the FSB was always big on blowing things up and then pointing their finger at the Chechens or Dagestanis. I think what happened was simply that people on our side saw how successful this was and decided to run their own scheme. When both sides found out, they started cooperating." On this topic, David knew he was on firm ground since he had written an entire analysis paper on it.

"So more like 'dictatorship of agencies.' Either you've come across the most hideous operation ever, or your brain has been replaced with some cancerous artifact that needs to be quickly composted. I can't really decide which."

"Yup, I felt the same way when I first heard. The real question is how do we get solid evidence?"

"Actually, I might have a way. There is someone you might remember from your past life who used to work for a company that sold Soviet raw materials to French aerospace companies. He was stationed in Montpellier for a while."

David's face brightened. "How the hell did you find Yuri?"

"He is retired and lives in Hyeres. Calls himself Frantisek now and pretends to be a former Polish naval officer."

"Does he know you?"

"I don't travel in his circles. He doesn't even know of me. I collect garbage for a living and clean the clubhouse of the golf course on the weekends. That's where I saw him one day and recognized him immediately."

"Why do you think he'd know about any of this?"

"Because he was talking to one of those newly rich Russians who hang out down here. My Russian is not that good, but I was able to figure out that he predicted the CIA would announce a foiled terror plot and that the Russians would support the news with evidence of their own. Two days later it happened exactly as Yuri predicted. At the time I didn't think much of it, but now that you mention all this, it kind of fits the story, doesn't it?"

"So he is not really retired."

"Do you know any agents who are retired and not dead?"

"So how do I talk to Yuri?"

"How is your golf game?"

"Sucks."

"Good. You'll get along fine then. Be on the golf course early morning. You can't miss him."

"When can we meet again?"

"There is a mosque not far from the beach. Have you seen it?"

"Yes."

"Meet me for Friday prayer tomorrow."

"So how was your meeting with your friend?"

"Not good. We will have to move."

"Where to? We can't go back to Turkey."

"Algeria might be best. We'd pass as Algerians who lived in France as long as we keep our heads down."

"I'm getting very tired of this."

"Me too. But I don't see how we have any choice."

"When are we leaving?"

"Could be any minute. But there is one thing I want to help him with first."

Her raised eyebrow made words unnecessary. *You really need that kind of risk for someone else?*

"He's a friend. One of the few people I trust."

David thought for a while about Yuri. He wasn't sure what his real name and identity were, but he knew him as Yuri Aranskiy. In the early 1980s they were both stationed in Montpellier. For David, it was his second assignment abroad, and he was supposed to keep in contact with a network around the Mediterranean. Yuri was a young aerospace engineer acting as a sales agent for a Soviet company trying to sell metals and minerals to French heavy industry. His real assignment was industrial espionage. They developed an awkward friendship at the time. Both knew what the other was doing, but neither would ever discuss it openly.

According to Erdal, he was somehow mixed up in a scheme that ran terror plots for the sole purpose of exposing them. He wasn't surprised that the FSB, the successor to the old KGB, would be involved in this. But Yuri had always seemed like a straight-up old-fashioned spy.

Talking to him would be tricky. If he were really involved in this, Yuri would likely sell him out to the CIA the moment David brought up the topic. Probably better to stay away from him. Or maybe there was a way...

"Nora, I will need to go to Aix-en-Provence tomorrow. Do you think you can get us a car?"

"No problem. What's in Aix?"

"Regional headquarters of the DCRI."

"And you'll just waltz in assuming they won't arrest you just because you're officially dead?"

"The director is Jean Renard. Every day at 12:15, he walks home two blocks, has lunch with his wife and her disabled sister, then he goes back to his office. I'll visit an old friend. And I'm counting on the director to remember he still owes me."

"You're serious then. What do you think he can do for you?"

"Help me with a former KGB officer."

"Are we talking about Yuri Aranskiy?"

David did not show his surprise. "Yes, I need to find out what he's up to, and I might need someone to grill him—the French secret service has jurisdiction around here."

"I might be able to get you a head start. Aranskiy has left the KGB over ten years ago. Since then he has been selling his services to Russian oligarchs trying to do business in the Mediterranean or trying to find safe locations for their money. He is rumored to keep good relations with more than one agency, including very good connections inside DCRI. To the outside world he displays a strong distaste for the new leadership of the FSB, but many think it's just an act. He has been associated with some pretty unsavory elements here in southern France. People who know him well call him—"

"The crocodile, yes," David interjected, "because he snaps at everything around him and never lets go. Plus his dental work might have something to do with it."

"So you know him."

"He and I spent some quality time in Montpellier, mostly opposing each other, sometimes horse trading."

"What are you hoping to get from him?"

"Insight on how terror plots are arranged as a show for the public to justify more funding and more influence for the secret services."

"So you are starting to believe the story?"

"Apparently, Yuri has been predicting specific cases before they happened."

"Could mean he's involved, or he has a front seat."

"Right, but talking to him is dangerous since he knows me."

"But he doesn't know me."

FRIDAY, EARLY MORNING. VALGARDE GOLF COURSE.

She had been hitting golf balls for almost half an hour before a group of people showed up. She got a good look at all four members of the group—no sign of Aranskiy. After another twenty minutes, he showed up with two bodyguards and an apparently well-established routine: the two pit bulls checked the sign-in sheet, noticed the group of four and recognized the names, then saw a new name and looked in her direction when the kid at the entrance pointed her out. She smiled back at them trying to look harmless. After that the pit bulls were satisfied that there was no threat and placed themselves at the bar while Aranskiy started his game.

Nora made sure she crossed paths with Aranskiy once he was out of sight of the coffee bar where his pit bulls had started the morning with vodka shots. She saw his ball land near a sandpit and shot her own ball right into the pit. Then she arrived before him and had her shot ready just as he was lining up for his own. She hit the sand hard enough to have her ball roll out of the pit slowly, accompanied by a spray of sand that hit Aranskiy.

"Merde—since when do they let women play here anyways?"

"Je suis désolée, monsieur."

"You better be sorry. I'll get you thrown out of this joint."

By this time she had caught up with him. "Don't move. I have a sniper sitting up in the tree. One wrong move and you'll fertilize the grass." David pulled his hoodie more tightly over his face and waved, hoping Yuri would accept the iron bar he was carrying as a gun—given the distance, probably a reasonable bet.

"What do you want? If you wanted to kill me, you could have already done so."

"And I still might. But first, I'd like to know how you figured out that there would be a car bomb in the Garden State Plaza Mall in New Jersey, and that it would be found before it blew up."

"I'm not talking to little kids, especially not girls, and most certainly not about topics that are for grown-ups only."

With a quick swing, her golf club hit his kneecap—hard enough to be extremely painful, but just short of breaking any bones. He fell to the ground and stared up at her in disbelief. "You'll be fine after a few days unless you keep misbehaving."

"You'll pay for this—messing with me is not healthy."

"Shut up. People who mess with me end up dead. I guess that makes us some sort of evil twins, eh? So listen Monsieur

Aranskiy—you still call yourself that, don't you?—we already know a fair amount about you. You are selling secret information to Russian oligarchs so that they can front-run the news with their investments."

"Who is the 'we'?"

"None of your fucking business." The swear word was accompanied by another blow of the golf club, this time lighter and on the wrist.

"So since when is dealing with inside information a problem?"

"Since we say so."

"Get a grip. If you think I'm letting you play in this field, you're dreaming."

She realized she was not getting anywhere. "I'm not here to shut you down or take over your business. I don't even care about your contacts inside the FSB—although I suspect I may know them better than you do and could get them to drop you any time I say. What I'm here for is proof. I want independent confirmation of what we've learned through other channels."

He smiled. "You want to become a customer. You could have just said so. Normally this is by recommendation only, but I might make an exception for you. Only, what do I get out of it?"

She let her golf club dangle a little more and said, "For starters, you might improve your orthopedic health. We might even let you live. Most importantly, you would help us turn the secret services back to what they are supposed to do."

She watched his reaction carefully. David had been right: Yuri was indeed an old-fashioned spy, and the thought of pulling a fast one on the new guard who had taken over what he thought had once been an honorable industry seemed to amuse him. "I'm actually starting to like you. What are you doing for lunch?"

She rolled her eyes.

"Seriously. Every day at noon, I take a quick midday drink at Le Papaya down near the port. Be there today. I'll have a little present for you."

"I will."

"One more thing: I will be accompanied by two of my associates. Muscular types—you might have noticed them. Don't bring your golf clubs."

"I will not be alone either. You will not notice who is with me, but your pit bulls better stay leashed."

David was worried: "We know nothing about Le Papaya—it could easily be an ambush."

"David, you said so yourself: he is likely intrigued by the idea of reining in the new guard at the FSB."

"Except not with someone he doesn't know at all and who just humiliated him by beating him up on a golf course. Maybe I should show up instead."

"No way, especially if we are not sure about his intentions yet. He knows me now, and he agreed to meet with me. I will go."

"What's our plan if he is setting this up as a trap?"

"I think we simply do not have any alternatives. We either cut this short or we do it as it is set up."

"Promise me one thing: don't be shy about sounding the emergency signal." David didn't like it but he had no other ideas.

David settled into a pizzeria across the street an hour before the meeting. He relaxed a bit when he did not see any preparations going on at Le Papaya. If Yuri were sending an advance team, there would have to be some sign of it. If he were up to something, he'd likely have his pit bulls set up a trap. Nora arrived at 11:45 and sat at one of the window tables as they had discussed. There was barely any traffic in the bar.

Yuri arrived exactly at noon with his two bodyguards in tow. After they entered the bar, he could no longer see the bodyguards, but Yuri was sitting alone with Nora next to the window.

"Glad you could make it, Monsieur Aranskiy. How is your knee?"

Yuri chose not to answer. Instead, he got settled in his seat across the table. He put some papers on the table between them, fiddled with something under the table, and said, "Let's get to business. You'll notice that the people you call my 'pit bulls' are not in the room. One is in the back by the restrooms, the other at the rear entrance in a car. The owner behind the bar is my employee. He has been instructed to clear this room so that we can have some privacy. As we speak, his waiters are helping the last customers outside since a private event is starting in a few minutes—at least that is the story he is telling."

Nora knew immediately that this did not bode well.

"I suspect your team is watching from across the street, which is why you have chosen a window seat. In case you are getting any ideas, the waiter at the door is armed, and I'm holding a gun under the table and am ready to fire it right into your stomach if you make one wrong move."

"So where are we going? Cause if you wanted to kill me, you could have done so by now."

"Good observation. You will excuse yourself to go to the bathroom. You will be escorted to my car in the back where I will join you momentarily. Are we clear?"

"Very much so."

Chapter 5

David saw people exiting Le Papaya and saw through the window how Nora got up from the table. She looked across the street at him briefly before she walked away toward the bathrooms. Yuri collected the papers on the table and followed her. David knew the operation had failed. Normally protocol would have dictated to abandon and let someone else deal with the fallout. In this case, however, there was nobody else and he had to improvise.

Erdal had told him Yuri's address, on the peninsula south of the harbor. So he decided to walk down and simply knock on the door.

One of the pit bulls opened and seemed to expect, if not him, then at least someone. He checked him for weapons and led him into the backyard.

"David? Aren't you supposed to be dead?"

"Can't kill an old dog like me that easily." He looked around and saw Nora tied up on a chair. She was bleeding from a head wound and was covered in bruises across the face. The second pit bull was standing next to her rubbing his right fist.

"Am I correct that you are here to talk to me about your friend?"

"Yes, I was hoping to talk some sense into everybody." Nora threw him a look that seemed to say *get out while you can*.

"I must say, I am extremely disappointed. Since when do you need to send a children's army after me? I thought we had a better relationship than that. David, why didn't you come talk to me?"

"Not that easy—after all, I'm dead." He remembered that Yuri didn't exactly have a sense of humor, so he added, "Look, just cut her a break—all she did was try to establish contact in a way that can't be traced to me in case it fails."

"Is that really all? I think you forgot the part where she threatened me, tried to kneecap me, and worst of all disturbed my golf game. I never liked violence, but I learned to live with it. But you just don't mess with golf." He poured a glass from a tall bottle and offered David one: "Sto gram?"

David took the vodka glass and held it up. "To old times?"

"To deception and influence."

"Deception and influence."

"So I take it you met Lolek and Bolek."

"Lolek and Bolek?"

"That's what I call them. I can't pronounce these Polish names, so I had to find something simpler."

"Before we start talking, can you please let her go? She is as much part of this as I am."

"Then you better explain yourself. Here, take this knife and cut her lose yourself."

As he did, the pit bull was watching suspiciously. David looked at the damage to Nora's face closely but didn't see anything that wouldn't heal within a few weeks. She got up from the chair, and before David realized what was happening, she drove her fist into the pit bull's face, hitting his nose from below.

"Aaaaaghh. She bwoke my nohse!!"

Yuri jumped up to break up the fight. "Lolek, stop. Bolek, take him out back and get him some ice." And turning to Nora, "You are some naughty little bitch." David knew him well enough to recognize a shade of respect in the insult.

When they were alone, Yuri came straight to the point: "What the hell happened to you? Don't tell me you are here on official business."

David thought it over and then decided to come clean— mostly anyways. "When we both worked in Montpellier, we were on different sides. We had different interests. We did our best to defeat the other and sometimes we found it in the best of both our interests to trade."

"And occasionally we stole from each other."

"Part of the game as we knew it. We did engage in deception either to obtain information or to seed misinformation. But I always had the sense that we respected each other and wouldn't do things to create unnecessary harm."

"Yes, but they don't run things this way anymore."

"I am painfully aware of that. As you probably know, I officially died in a bomb attack that was conducted by the very group that I successfully infiltrated."

"Bullshit. I knew immediately this could not be true. This would require your field agent to be a double agent, and if they really turned him, why kill the golden goose? Plus, counterintelligence in these terrorist groups barely exists. And one more thing: your agent wouldn't have turned up here in the south of France if he had just blown up his handler."

This was a surprise. "You knew?"

"We had our own agent in the group and we suspected Erdal to be someone else's—and guess what, once we looked, your name came up. And then wouldn't you know, a couple of months later, I see his ugly mug here in the street."

It took David a few minutes to process this piece of news. He decided to continue. "I have reasons to believe that the hit was real and meant for me. But I need help figuring out what is really going on."

Yuri thought for a while before answering. "So you decided to take on the CIA's apparatchiks with a little kid and an old man as your army?"

David looked sheepish.

"David, look—I think you know how I make a living these days and what my interests are. I will not rat you out, but I can't be part of this."

"No need to get involved. I'm only asking for your insights."

Yuri thought it over for a few minutes before he continued speaking. "You're right. When we first got to know each other, we were running what I still think of as a respectable spy business. Even the French would simply watch us, knowing they'd win occasionally, lose some, and in general continue to play the game and learn a thing or two.

"After the Soviet Union collapsed, I was asked to start working for the FSB, which was initially pretty much the same as the old KGB. I was in the foreign directorate, my boss stayed the same, life was good. But things changed almost fifteen years ago. The war in Chechnya wasn't going anywhere and the Russian public was getting extremely tired of it. So someone decided to give Russians a little scare to boost their commitment. We blew up apartment buildings, placed bombs in railway stations, defused some, and let others blow up—David, we actually killed people in the process, and nobody thought this was wrong. Then we declared it all the work of Chechen separatists. It worked beautifully. Everybody bought the story, and public opinion completely turned the way we wanted it. It was disgusting. I knew better than to question things, and I didn't have to: people were openly wisecracking about how we had stuck it to the Chechens. I have no idea whether this is true, but word inside the FSB was that this was all done with direct knowledge of the Kremlin.

"I retired from the FSB a year later and started a consulting business. Occasionally the FSB is using my service, but more frequently my customers are the people in Russia who profit from current events. My former colleagues know when and where terror plots are about to be 'discovered.' I allow a small number of people to profit from the information."

"But all this is inside Russia?"

"No. I get information on so-called terror plots anywhere in the world."

"They can't all be instigated by the FSB then."

"Correct. I never asked who exactly is involved. But the CIA definitely is, the British have a stake in it, and there appear to be a couple of other players. In each country it works the same way: whichever agency works in the most clandestine fashion is the one that participates, while everybody else is kept unaware. Plots are being cooked up centrally. In most cases, they use some active cell, usually bloody amateurs who would not be able to pull anything this large off. They infiltrate the cell, often months in advance. The agent acts as a true provocateur, suggests the attack, supplies all the material, gets everybody motivated, and is by all accounts the sole ringleader. But he manages to get someone else to think he is in charge and to take full credit, which really means taking the fall. So when the group gets busted, he either goes down with it and gets convicted in court before he vanishes into witness protection or he splits from the group before they get picked up.

"So law enforcement never is aware of this being a CIA or FSB operation; they just enjoy their pat on the back for busting a terror operation just before it happened. Some people might ask where the tip was coming from and how they got so lucky. Usually the answer is something along the lines of 'electronic surveillance—we should not talk about it too much.' But the truth is everybody is treating this whole business as if it were real. In the meantime, they all forget that they were supposed to be the intelligence arm of their respective countries to give them an advantage over the other guys. When we were still in the game, that's what we cared about, didn't we?"

"I'd like to think it's still like that."

"You're dreaming then. Both your agency and mine have found ways to ask for more influence and money, both of which they will then use to create a threat potential that is unrelated to the real world and gets set up only for one purpose: to ask for even more money and influence. A true vicious cycle. It is no longer CIA against KGB, it is each agency against their own governments."

"So then, how come none of this came out when Edward Snowden defected and released his secret documents?"

"The NSA is not in on the plot, not officially. They only benefit from it. And the Snowden thing presented the FSB with a real dilemma. They had to play their part in opposing the US, but they were deadly afraid that he might have information about the stuff we are talking about here. As it turned out, Snowden had plenty of information to embarrass everybody, but nothing that was truly dangerous. The way it works is that the CIA gets to set things up, and then they leak selectively to law enforcement using so-called secret NSA information that cannot be disclosed publicly. Law enforcement is grateful, and usually able to handle things on their own given the leads. Then when things blow up, they are the heroes and give some of the credit back to the CIA who uses it to say 'see—that's why we need Congress to hand us more money and to stop asking questions.' Everybody feels protected and gives the CIA what they want."

"And nobody questions this?"

"Certainly not in Russia or Britain. From what I'm hearing, in the US some people have tried. Congressmen who asked pointed questions found that the CIA knew about certain activities of theirs and was ready to expose them for crimes they thought they had swept under the rug, sexual misconduct they thought nobody knew about, or in some cases things they had nothing to do with but where proof could be manufactured. And suddenly, they were far less interested in exposing the CIA."

"Blackmailing Congress? That's an extremely dangerous game. But none of this explains why I was simply parked for five years. If they wanted me out of the way, they should have killed me. And if they needed me for something, why didn't I hear anything?"

"Well, you might not be as important as you thought—has it occurred to you they might have forgotten that you exist?"

"I have weekly calls with our retirement handlers and they check everything I do."

Yuri looked alarmed, but didn't say anything.

"Don't worry—after five years I have figured out how to defeat their controls. I managed to be absent for extended periods before without detection."

"The other possibility is that they might have expected you to take some action by yourself. Depending on what they expect you to do, they will sooner or later come and ask directly."

"This might be about to happen. I was told that I'm supposed to be reactivated."

"Then you should listen to them and find out what they want from you. If I had to guess, I'd say there is unfinished business in your past that's too delicate for them to touch without you."

David thought about this for a while but there was nothing he could remember. Then it hit him.

Yuri noticed: "You look like a train just hit you."

"I think I just remembered. We'll need to go. One question: Is there any terror plot about to be exposed?"

"If I knew, why would I tell you?"

"For old times' sake. And to uphold the honor of the real spies."

"Nothing I know for sure. But I would say don't go shopping in Minnesota next week."

As they were walking back to their hotel, David said, "I'm sorry. I should have insisted on going myself. I should not have put you in this position."

"Bullshit. It was the right way to do it, and you know it as well as I do. Thanks for coming after me, though. I think we know a fair amount more about Yuri now, but if I were in your shoes, I'd want to know how deep this goes in the CIA."

You mean you'd want me to spy on the CIA to find out which departments the Mossad can still do business with and which ones to stay away from. Aloud he said, "There's only one way to find out. I will have to let them reactivate me. But first I need to talk to Erdal tonight."

He arrived at the mosque just before the service started. He left his shoes at the entrance and looked around, but when he spotted Erdal, he was walking toward a different door at the side of the building. He put his shoes back on and followed. He tried the door but found it locked. He knocked, still wondering why Erdal had told him to meet at prayer service rather than in the adjacent building when the door opened and he was staring at a gun with a silencer.

It was dark when he woke up and found himself tied up in the back of a van driving on what felt like side streets and cobblestone. First he could not see anything, but gradually his eyes got used to the dark. He was alone in the van with one other person who seemed to be tied up as well. He nudged the other person with his feet, which produced a groan. Gradually Erdal was sitting up.

"What happened?"

"I was hoping you would not see me. They told me they have Yasemin and the kids and I had to show up in the building next to the mosque at 5:30."

"Who are they?"

"Not sure, but they sounded Russian or some other Eastern European variety."

"How did they find you?"

"By following your trail, I'm pretty sure."

David had to admit he could not rule out that someone would have followed him. He did not have enough time to scout the meeting places as carefully as he would have liked. But he was pretty sure only one other person knew exactly where he was.

Nora had watched the mosque from a grocery store across the street. When she saw David go inside only to emerge a few minutes later, she thought something had gone wrong. Then she saw him following someone into the house next door and figured the meeting had been moved. She watched the house for a while before a van pulled up next to the door and blocked her view. Since David had expected to meet with one person, she figured someone else must have joined the party, and she needed to find out what was going on. She walked past the van and attached a magnetic GPS device inside the wheel well.

Seeing a group of men loading the van with heavy things she could not see clearly from afar, she decided to wait and take a closer look at the house once the van was gone.

There was nothing to see—no signs of a struggle, no people, no David, and no Erdal. There was only one conclusion: this was an ambush and David was in the van. She returned to the hotel and started checking the van's path on her control screen. It had not gone far and was parked at a hotel called Lingousto in the small town of Pierrefeu, which also had a private airport. She figured it was time to take a look.

The van had stopped. They heard voices outside but could not understand what was being said. After about twenty minutes of listening to footsteps going back and forth, some shouting, and doors being opened and slammed, someone opened the back door of the van and pointed a light directly at David's face. "Get out."

They were brought inside what looked like a small country hotel and were forced to walk into the basement. He counted four people with guns and another two in the background. There was no sign of the hotel staff.

They were locked into a pantry for a while before the door opened and two armed, masked men joined them. One of them started talking in heavily accented French. "We are sorry to inconvenience you. But we are looking for information that we think only you can provide. So we do not have any other choice but to ask you to come with us. Tomorrow morning a small airplane will arrive and take you to a place where you can safely disclose what you know. If we are satisfied, we will then bring you back here and you can go wherever you please."

"So you plan to abduct us to a place where you can torture and interrogate us."

"Please! We would never suggest anything like that. You will be our guests and we definitely hope you will enjoy the trip."

"Then why the guns?"

"Only because we need to insist you do exactly as we say."

"So where are we going?"

"A town called Urus-Martan."

"In Chechnya."

"Yes."

"Why don't you ask us right here? If I can help, I will tell you what you need to know and we can all be on our way by tomorrow morning."

"I'm afraid this won't work. I'm not the one who knows what to ask. And besides, we are not interested in you. It's your friend that we are supposed to bring. You just joined the party."

"So I take it you are not affiliated with the FSB?"

The second armed man who had not said a word started chuckling until the speaker threw him a look that froze his laugh. "You can safely assume we do not wish to be mistaken for KGB thugs."

When Nora arrived at Lingousto, she saw the van in the parking lot. No other cars were present, and she saw only one light that seemed to come from the basement. For a moment she thought of walking into the reception and asking for a room. But with the building looking abandoned, she decided to check things from the outside.

She walked around the hotel trying to find a window or any other opening to look inside, but all the ground-floor windows were dark, and the light coming from the basement was from a hallway that appeared empty. After a while she heard noises on the other side of the building and went to check what was going on. Three men were walking out of the main entrance talking to each other. She was not close enough to understand what was said but it appeared to be the night watch being set up. Staying was too dangerous; she had to retreat and call for help.

For the rest of the night, she kept watching the hotel from a safe distance.

David had tried to get Erdal to tell him what he thought was going on and why a group of Chechens wanted to interrogate him, but he either did not know or was unwilling to talk. So by morning all he knew was that he was going to Chechnya on a trip that he was initially not invited on. Clearly this was not good. But at least it was neither the CIA nor the FSB, so he figured Erdal must have somehow stepped on the Chechens' toes, or maybe it was all just a big misunderstanding. Somehow, however, he figured that in the world he moved in, there wasn't a lot of room for casual misunderstandings.

As the first light came through the window, David heard cars and shouting outside, and he looked at Erdal who was just as puzzled. After a while Erdal started grinning and said, "It's a tax raid."

"You have to be kidding. What are the odds?"

The French tax authorities were well aware of the habit of hotel owners to underreport their bookings. So occasionally, they showed up for early morning visits where they asked to see the registration books and compared them with the actual room occupancy. These visits were very rare, but most hotel owners lived in fear of being caught in one of them. Usually, they involved lots of police and severe dissatisfaction for the hotel guests who were woken up early in the morning.

At the front desk, a very rude tax officer rang the bell and asked to see the registration book. The person who answered him in broken French did not understand what was going on but saw police with guns and decided it was time to wake up his boss.

The tax officer was getting very impatient and started sending his team through the hotel rooms to count how many were occupied. When the hotel manager showed up, he spoke to the person who woke him in a language the tax officer did not understand, then turned around and asked how he could help.

"For starters, I'd like to see your registration book."

"I don't know why you came here today—we are closed for the entire week while we are renovating. There is not a single entry in the book."

"So if we look through your rooms, we will not find anybody staying there?"

"Only the contractors who are helping me paint the walls."

"Monsieur!" One of the policemen had found the basement door locked.

"I can't open this door for you."

"Then I'm afraid we might have to do it for you."

After a short standoff, the hotel manager found the key and opened the basement door. Two policemen went down and a few minutes later returned with David and Erdal, still in hand-cuffs.

In the meantime, Nora kept watching the van in the parking lot and saw four men getting in and driving off at high speed. She decided to let them go for now and figure out later whether or not to pass their location to the police. She was reasonably sure that David was not in the van.

The tax officer raised an eyebrow when he heard how the police had found David and Erdal. He turned to the hotel manager and said, "I thought you ran a hotel here, not a prison."

"I do not know who these people are and how they got here."

"Monsieur, someone just left in a hurry, and we found two rooms that were occupied overnight."

"I suspect you'll try to convince me those were your painters?"

"As I said, I have never seen these two before, and yes, I do have four painters in the house. They share two rooms on the upper floor."

"We found guns and rope in the rooms they stayed in, but no paintbrushes and no paint. Are you sure this is your story?"

"As I said..."

"Well, it's probably best you clear this up with the police."

He turned to David and Erdal to find out what they had to say. After a long and uncomfortable discussion, David managed to convince the police that this had to be a case of mistaken identity. They were sitting in a café late last night when a van pulled up and they were thrown inside by masked men who called them "Henry" and "Karim"—clearly not their names—and wanted to know about two other people they had never heard about. No, they did not want to press charges. If the police could find the men with the van or maybe warn Henry and Karim, it would certainly be nice. But they had not been hurt, and aside from the nightly detour they had no reason to complain.

One of the policemen offered to drive them where they needed to be, and David gave him an address in Toulon thinking they'd make their way back to Hyeres once they had been dropped off.

Nora got into the car she had borrowed from the hotel manager at the Hotel du Soleil and followed the police car to Toulon.

Once it had left, she picked up David and Erdal to drive them back to Hyeres.

David asked: "So I suspect we owe you a big thank-you for orchestrating a tax raid?"

She just smiled.

"How did you pull this off?"

"Not by myself. I had to call in a few favors. But someone in my office has had dealings with your friendly tax officer in the past and asked him to take a look at a building in Pierrefeu."

"How did you know where to look for us?"

"I was watching the mosque, saw the van, figured it was a little suspicious, and put a tracker on it."

"A tracker? Is it still on the van?"

"Yes."

"I'm impressed."

"Not to ruin the celebration, but I still have a huge problem." Erdal seemed distressed. "Remember, they have my family, and I'd much rather follow them to Chechnya and tell them what they want to know than risk Yasemin's and the kids lives."

"Chechnya? What are you talking about?" Nora was puzzled.

"We have reason to believe that we were supposed to be taken to Urus-Martan to be questioned by a Chechen group that is fighting the Russians. They kidnapped Erdal's wife and children to pressure him into going. I was just the accidental bystander."

"How do we know they are kidnapped? And why do you think it helps that you go where they say?"

Erdal was still worried, bordering on panicked. "They are missing and I have little reason to doubt them."

"Okay, but what makes you think caving to their demands will make a difference?" Nora was doing her best to get Erdal to treat the situation from the point of view of a hostage expert, but Erdal remained the panicked husband and caring father.

David decided to jump in. "If they do have them, would we assume that the van is going where they keep them? I don't see a bunch of Chechens running a huge operation in the South

of France—even the hotel hideout seemed rather cobbled together. I would guess that they only have a single safe house
and the van is going right there."

"Unless it's going to the airport to meet whoever was supposed to pick us up and deliver my family instead."

"Here—check it on my cell phone. The tracker app is called
'T.'" Nora was back to all business and rationality.

David checked the movement of the van and saw that it had
gone from the Lingousto straight to the local airport and it had
not moved in the last hour. They decided to go check on it.

When they arrived at the tiny airfield, the van was parked
across the street and appeared empty. There were no airplanes
on the landing strip, only a couple of small private airplanes
that were tied down. They walked into the office and asked
whether any airplanes had come in this morning. The woman
behind the desk said "only this crazy flight from Tirana—they
wanted to buy fuel immediately so that they could turn around.
Told me they had made a mistake with their route and had to
turn around before they'd get into trouble with air traffic control. Boy, were they in a hurry."

"Tirana you said?"

"Yes, in Albania. It was a twin-engine Cessna, one of those
six-seaters—probably just enough fuel to make it there one
way."

"Did anybody get on the plane?"

"No, they can't pick up passengers here."

"But could somebody have walked onto the airfield without
you knowing it?"

She seemed startled as to why anybody would want to do
this but admitted, "We don't have a lot of security here—if they
walk in, nobody would stop them. Why?"

"Oh, there is a van outside that had four people in it earlier
and we are wondering where they are."

"Are you with the police or something?"

"No, just looking for our friends."

"Well, your friends are a little strange—and they seem to be in a huge hurry. But they did not get on the Tirana flight. Although they did talk to the pilot now that you mention it."

"And where did they go after that?"

"I think they are still somewhere out on the airfield. I didn't see them leave."

At that moment, shouting started outside, and she turned around to see what was going on. Her eyes widened, and she picked up the radio. "Flight F-AGEH—you are NOT cleared for takeoff. Please clear the runway immediately." She repeated the announcement a few times along with requests for confirmation. But instead of a confirmation, the airplane accelerated and took off. "Merde."

While everybody was watching the plane take off, Erdal noticed the TV behind the desk switching to local news. An apartment building in Hyeres had burned down and police suspected arson and were looking for one of the residents as their primary suspect. He recognized the neighborhood and did not need the newscaster to confirm Rue Saint-François as the address.

On the drive back from the airport, Erdal spoke up. "Please drop me at the Hyeres police station."

David gave him a suspicious look. "What's going on?"

"My apartment burned down and police are looking for me. They think I set the fire."

"We can clear this up; we know where you were."

"Except you can't even identify yourself without explaining why you're not dead, and I'm not sure how much of her identity Nora is willing to reveal."

Her look made it perfectly clear that Nora's identity was not to be disclosed to French police.

"What do you think police will do—aside from arresting you?"

"At least they can start looking for my family."

"You'll need to start thinking logically. The apartment burned last night while they had us tied up?"

"Yes, late afternoon."

"What could be the reason they would do this? My guess is they were bluffing about having abducted your family. The Chechens probably showed up at your apartment and either Yasemin saw them and ran or she just wasn't there. So they made sure she would not come back, giving them a time window where you would not be able to contact her."

"No cell phone?" Nora seemed unconvinced.

"Turning off her cell phone is the first thing Yasemin would do if she felt like someone was tracking her."

"So where do you think she might go?"

"We don't have a lot of friends here. Ahmad and his wife run an Algerian grocery store around the corner. Unless she thought it was too close to the house, it's the most likely place."

As they entered the grocery store, Erdal greeted the owner with a quiet "Sala'am" while looking over his shoulder to see who else was in the store. Ahmad nodded toward the back door, and when David and Nora tried to follow, he held out a hand to stop them. Erdal signaled that it was okay.

In the back, Ahmad whispered, "Police are looking for you. What happened?"

"What did you tell them?"

"Nothing. Just that I last saw you in the morning when you came in for coffee before taking off for work. What did you get yourself involved in? You know French police—they don't like us and are looking for any excuse to blame us for whatever they can." Ahmad sounded like a nervous wreck.

David jumped in. "It's not him. I suspect I am the one who started the trouble. It's a little complicated to explain, but right now we need to make sure Yasemin and the kids are okay."

"They are staying at my mother's house. You know where it is?"

"Yes."

"Mehdi, be careful. The police seem to think you set the fire at your house. I know you didn't, but watch out."

"I will."

It took David a second to remember that Erdal was living under a false identity. When they walked out he said, "You're able to pass as one of theirs among Algerians? I'm impressed."

"My mother is Algerian. She used to speak only Arabic to me. I don't speak any of the regional languages so I can't pretend that I grew up in Algeria. But my story is that I'm of Algerian descent and spoke Arabic with my parents while growing up in France. Close enough to the truth."

They found Erdal's family in a worried state and decided to bring everybody to the hotel du Soleil to figure out what to do.

David advocated a wait-and-see approach: "No, you cannot go to the police. What would you tell them? 'Yes, I know you think I set the fire, but I was actually busy being abducted by a group of Chechens who have since stolen an airplane and probably left the country by now.' Do you know how ridiculous this sounds?"

"The police from the tax raid at the hotel where they held us would be able to confirm the story."

"Sure. Do you remember how we convinced them that there was really no need to keep our contact information and that we had definitely no plans to press charges. They might remember us, but they didn't check our identity—which by the way was precisely what we wanted—and they would probably start getting very suspicious when we show up again, this time to ask their help identifying us in conjunction with an arson investigation."

"We are four people. Six, if you count yourselves. We can't all stay in this tiny hotel room. Plus, it's too public—we'd be found within a day or two." Yasemin started to think analytically about the situation.

"My sister-in-law owns an apartment in a ski area not far from here," David said. "It is completely abandoned during the summer, and nobody will look for you there." David wasn't actually sure whether Elana's sister still owned the place, but he figured it was their best bet.

"Can you contact her?" Erdal had a good point.

"No, she thinks I'm dead. But there is no need. The apartment is managed by a local real estate agent. As long as they get an e-mail that looks like it comes from the owner, they will open it for you."

"So all we have to do is spoof the mail header and get it to route through a respectable mail relay to avoid being dropped in the spam folder." Clearly Nora had done this before.

"Pretty much."

Nora opened her laptop. "You have the e-mail address of the real estate agent?"

"No, but as I remember it, there are only two in the area. I will call to find out which one manages the apartment, then we can find their e-mail address with the help of Google."

As it turned out, there were now three real estate offices in the town of Valberg and one in neighboring Guillaume. One call to the tourism office confirmed that René Beauliard at Agence Valberg managed all the slope-side apartments in the ski resort.

Once all the arrangements were made, Erdal took David aside and said, "Before I leave I need to fill you in on some more details."

"In the car on the way up?"

"I'd prefer nobody else hearing any of this."

David knew he mainly meant Nora, so he suggested a quick walk. It was risky since Erdal's face was all over the local news. But Hyeres was a sleepy tourist town, and the hotel was off the beaten track in the old city center and not far from a park where they could be reasonably certain that they would not meet a lot of people in the midday heat.

Nora raised an eyebrow when she heard they were planning to go out. "With every cop in this city looking for him?" But she knew she would not be able to keep them from going. Yasemin was equally worried but said nothing.

"So what is it that Nora could not hear?"

"Remember I told you that on the day after the bomb exploded at your house, Hani, the leader of the cell, came to ask me about you?"

"Yes, I suspect that is because my name was associated with the attack?"

"Well, that's just it. The news was only talking about 'a senior CIA agent.' It took another two weeks before they identified you."

"So you think Hani knew of our connection?"

"That's what I thought at the time and it was the reason why we left town immediately. But there was more that he said at the time."

David looked at Erdal, who seemed tortured about what he had to say.

"Hani mentioned that you were the author of a CIA report that analyzed the latest changes at the FSB and how they created and instigated threat potentials for the purpose of entrapment and to profit from the raised threat level. He also said your report came to the conclusion that the CIA should install a similar program."

"If Hani did not know that I was your handler, he probably suspects it now. The other question is how did he obtain this information?"

"So it is true?"

"The first part yes. I wrote the analysis. My recommendation was a different one, though, but I suspect as the report made its way through the chain of approvals, its tone might have changed."

"I think Hani was likely the representative of another agency in the cell."

"Likely the FSB's given the nature of his information."

"Or Mossad. Or the DCRI."

"Maybe, but less likely. Neither the Israelis nor the French know about these details. But according to Yuri, the FSB and the CIA are cooperating on the topic."

"Which would also explain why the Chechens are showing up asking for explanations."

"Can't blame them—they are the losers in this whole scheme, aren't they?"

"You don't really think they would have asked us questions and then sent us back, do you?"

"Nonsense. We were scheduled to be tortured and then likely executed publicly as CIA agents who tried to infiltrate a group of Chechen freedom fighters. Or something very close to that story line. We are lucky that they can't mount a full-scale operation for a small target like us."

"They will try again though. Hopefully they will not be able to figure out who you are. Otherwise it will be with substantially increased effort."

David thought about this for a while. Erdal was right. They clearly had no idea who he was or they would have reacted very differently. They thought Erdal was the primary target and didn't know they had stumbled on something even more valuable. To Erdal he said, "So what else did Hani say at the time?"

"A couple of things that didn't make any sense then, but in the light of recent events, it's all different. He said he thought there was no attack."

"He is actually wrong on that. My house was destroyed and my wife was killed."

"Did you see her? And did you see the house?"

"I spoke to a firefighter who had sealed off my street and told me my house had been leveled by a bomb. My wife's body was burned beyond recognition."

"Officially, so was yours, right? So you don't really know."

"I suppose it could have been staged. But then why go through all the trouble?"

"Not for your benefit—for the public's."

David had to admit that he had arrived at similar suspicions in the last few days. But what Erdal was hinting went into far too outrageous territory. "It still does not explain who set all this up. I know my own agency is a prime suspect here, but I'm not really willing to buy this."

"Me neither. I suspect it was a joint operation by factions in both the FSB and the CIA who cooperated in an attempt to seize control in their respective agencies. And from recent events, I would say they seem to have succeeded."

"That would be a truly scary thought."

"But it fits the picture. I think the reason why Hani came to me was because he knew I was CIA. He might not have known about our connection, but he was probably hoping to enlist me for whichever faction he was part of. If you had to assess the people you know at the CIA and decide which side they are likely on, do you think you'd know?"

"Unlikely. Even the ones I know best play their cards extremely close to the chest."

"I am pretty sure by now Hani was looking for allies in a cross-agency struggle of factions. Problem is, I still don't know which side he was on."

"Yuri might know." David was a little uncomfortable mentioning Yuri given their latest interactions, but he had to admit he'd be a prime source.

"Yes, but depending on which side Yuri is on, there is a ton of misinformation he might choose to plant."

"So any other hints you picked up from Hani?"

"Only one more thing that appeared as strange at the time as it is now. When he was leaving, he said, 'If you ever hear anything about something called the Anderssen Gambit, keep your distance and let me know.' Do you have any idea what this could be?"

David had heard the name before. The German chess player Adolf Anderssen had made a name for himself with surprise attacks on his opponents that involved sacrifices of important pieces that looked too good to be true to his opponents—and that was exactly what they were, meant as bait to trick them into committing fatal mistakes that usually ended in checkmate a few moves ahead. Chess players called his technique a "sham sacrifice" since it was designed to create an advantage rather than being a real sacrifice.

His report on the FSB's activities was called the Anderssen Gambit because of the FSB's willingness to sacrifice lives for what they thought of as the greater good. After he had written his report, some people in the CIA were trying to morph it into an Anderssen-style game plan engineered to solidify the agency's power and to force foreign agencies into cooperation. He had been very vocal about his opposition and had resented his work being hijacked by what he thought were rogue elements inside the CIA—aggressive young ultraconservatives who were energized by the support they thought they had from neoconservative politicians of the post-9/11 era. By his assessment they were certainly not powerful enough to be a major force inside the agency, but they were a major pain in his daily work since he had to constantly argue things that he thought should be obvious. Now it seemed like they actually did more than just talk.

"I assume you know the obvious—an Anderssen sacrifice is a sham sacrifice in chess that is used to trick the other side to make a fatal mistake."

"I'm not a chess player, but yes, Wikipedia helped."

"I have run into an Anderssen plot as it relates to agency work, and it was the basis for the paper I wrote. I actually used it as the title for the paper. I argued against it at the time, but I can't be sure that it was not executed."

"So Hani's comment was a warning."

"I'd be willing to interpret it as one, yes."

"It would mean that he is part of the faction that would be considered friendly to our side in whichever agency he works."

"I think you are reading too much into it. Remember, agencies compete. We do everything including cutting a throat or two to get ahead of the other guys and gain a slight advantage for our side. They would do the same thing. The fact that both of us despise a world where we make up enemies because it has gotten too hard to track down the real bad guys the old-fashioned way doesn't make us allies."

Erdal seemed pained by what David thought was just a reiteration of plain and obvious facts of life in an agency.

"You seem pained by this. Did you have any more recent contact with Hani?"

"No. But I thought about what he had said since you showed up here and was trying to get my head around everything. So what did Yuri have to contribute on the topic?"

David sensed that there was more to the Hani story but decided to let it go. "Yuri confirmed that the FSB has indeed manufactured terror attacks and then blamed Chechen rebels. He also says this taught them that it is a viable strategy that works more generally and that it helps them solidify their power and influence in Russian society."

"As if that's necessary with a KGB colonel as their president."

"True enough. But more importantly, he seems to think there is a formal cooperation between the FSB and the CIA on the topic. He says the CIA analyzed the FSB strategy and decided they should follow the same model. I can confirm the first part since I was the one who wrote the book on it. But to imagine that the entire agency has gone rogue is incomprehensible to me. There are simply too many people involved who would speak up against it."

"It may not take a full consensus. You could run it on a small scale and do it by the use of a private channel with the Russians. It would almost be like a putsch inside the agency. People who were against it could still be blackmailed and made officially responsible for the outcome. And you could leave the majority of the agency in the dark. They would continue their work as before and not notice a thing."

David considered this for a while. As preposterous as it sounded at first, he had to admit this was indeed possible. "Do you have any hints that this is actually happening?"

"I have been even less involved than you for the last five years. But it sounds to me that everything is pointing in this direction, doesn't it?"

"Unfortunately yes. Yuri recommended I should let the CIA reactivate me to get a better idea of what is really going on."

"Any chance of that happening?"

"Henry called me a little more than a week ago and wanted me to be involved in some new stuff."

"Be careful then."

"I know. Let's get you and your family into your new mountain hideout first."

When they got back to the hotel, David immediately felt a sense of tension between Nora and Yasemin. He decided he needed to get to the bottom of it.

"Where did you get the car last night?"

"By flirting with the night manager so that he would let me use the hotel minivan."

"Is he back on duty yet?"

"Not sure. You want me to see if I can borrow it again?"

"Please."

After Nora left the room, David asked, "Everything all right between you two?"

"I don't understand why you are bringing the Israelis into this."

"There was no choice, Yasemin. They invited themselves and there was nothing I could do about it. But so far Nora has been extremely helpful."

"Let's hope she can keep her mouth shut about us."

"I will make sure of that."

Erdal was alarmed. "You are worried she might send the Mossad to the ski condo."

"Exactly."

David tried to calm their fears. "She does not have the address and I will drive you."

"But she helped make the connection with the real estate agent—all she has to do is ask him or send her friends to ask him."

"I guarantee you this will not happen, unless you want it to. Her boss has offered helping you start over with a new identity in exchange for information. But it would be completely up to you whether you want their help or not."

"And you're telling us now? How come you didn't mention this earlier?"

"I'm sorry—it was not top of my list. With yesterday's events, it now has a different urgency."

Erdal did not look convinced nor was he happy with what he had just heard. But David figured he'd come around.

Nora came back dangling car keys and said, "On y va?"

David was tempted to tell her to stay behind but decided against it. He figured it would be better to settle the Mossad's level of involvement with everybody in the car.

They decided to avoid the toll roads since they suspected security cameras might be mounted at the tollbooths and none of them wanted their faces to show up on anybody's facial recognition software. Instead, they took the local road through the hills behind the coastline toward Saint Tropez and Frejus. After they left the coastline at La Londe, the road led them through pine-covered sandy hills that had no resemblance to the usual Mediterranean coast until they saw the water again near Cogolin.

David wanted to make sure Nora knew to tread lightly with Erdal. "Nora, I know your organization is prepared to help Erdal and his family find a new identity. I just want to make sure we all understand you can offer, but it's up to them to decide."

"I've been asked to make sure he accepts the offer."

"I don't think you understand. If you insist and they don't like it, they will just vanish again. I believe they have proven their ability, and it took five years and my help to find them."

"I have my orders. I can't just ignore them."

"I know how agency hierarchies work—I've been part of them for a long time. Here's what you tell your boss: he can get my cooperation including my help convincing Erdal and his family to take your offer. But he will have to do without me, if he insists on accelerating the time line."

"So what is your proposed time line?"

"You don't bother them for the next two weeks. After that, they can decide." He was hoping that two weeks was enough to get to the bottom of this mess and have the answers he needed. After that, everybody could do whatever they wanted as far as he was concerned.

"In other words, we are facing a risk that the decision goes against us."

David was starting to get annoyed. He had not worked with such a junior agent in a long time. "Yes, and you have that very same risk right now. If you push too hard, they will be gone the moment you drop them off, and you will have no way to find them. Being patient is your only chance to get a yes."

"People will not be happy with this."

"Dial your phone and let me talk to them."

"I can't do that."

"Right now, or I stop the car and you can walk back to Hyeres."

She was clearly irritated but dialed her phone, then punched in a number and waited for the callback on a secure connection.

"David wants to talk to you."

"Monsieur Monthausser. What can I do for you?"

"It seems that we have arrived at a bit of a standoff here. My fellow agent that you have expressed an interest in deeply appreciates your offer of providing shelter for him and his family."

"Good. Can you bring him to one of our safe houses?"

"He is not ready to move that quickly. Don't forget he has a wife and two children, and rapidly changing their life plans is not something they can take lightly. We have found a temporary solution for them, and all we are asking is for you to give them two weeks to decide."

"What could possibly change within the next two weeks?"

"Nothing will change, but you need to let them make their own decisions without pressure."

"I understand there already was some pressure from a third party."

"Indeed, and I'm sure that weighs in your favor—especially with the help you provided. We were very impressed."

"Thank you. But keep in mind, favors are not free."

"I understand. And I'm trying to help you here. If you push too hard and too fast, you might not get what you want."

"So, it is two weeks before we establish contact?"

"Yes, please. And I assure you being patient will help your cause."

"David, you know we are a small country. We can't bully others and tell them what to do. In that spirit, let's talk in two weeks."

"Point taken. And thank you. One more question, if you have a second."

"Another favor? You are running deep into debt."

"This should be in our mutual interest. I believe you mentioned that you had a seat at the table in the group we had infiltrated."

"Complicated matter, but yes."

"I have reasons to think the person known as Hani was not your agent, but someone else's. Do you happen to know who he was working for at the time?"

A moment of silence was followed by, "We had our suspicions but were never able to confirm."

"Would you be able to share your suspicions?"

"The names MI6 and FSB were both in the running. Personally, I thought he was answering to the Russians, but if you are looking for hard information, I can't help."

"Fair enough; this is very helpful."

"Can you tell me why you are interested?"

"He has warned my contact using lingo that leads me to believe he has knowledge of deeply hidden documents at the CIA."

"Very interesting and I suppose supportive of the hypothesis you and I were discussing earlier."

"Indeed."

"Very well. If you have no further questions, au revoir, Monsieur Monthausser."

"Shalom."

Nora was fuming. But David didn't care. It was about time she learned how to navigate her own damn organization, he thought.

They turned north away from the coast in Sainte-Maxime, an old beach-resort town that had hosted the upper-class

Parisians in the summer months for many decades, and they cut through the hills and pine forests toward Draguignan and Castellane. The scenery started looking more and more alpine with white and light-gray rocks sticking out everywhere in the hills. After a left turn into a narrow canyon, the rocks turned into red limestone that looked almost shiny in the afternoon light. They navigated narrow roads, tunnels, and hairpin turns at slow speed for almost an hour before exiting the canyon in the town of Guillaumes, which was on a plateau that looked more like a temporary opening of the valley. In the town center, a group of bikers had just arrived and was taking a last break before continuing to follow the narrow valley to the Col de la Cayolle. David took a right turn instead, which quickly became a steep climb toward the small town of Valberg that was the closest ski resort for the more than a million people who lived in Nice and the surrounding areas.

David knew that Valberg was hopelessly overrun in the winter but almost completely dead in the summer aside from some locals and the occasional mountain biker. Elana's sister had bought an apartment here after her divorce from her arrogant but comfortably rich Wall Street banker husband, thinking she'd love to use it to ski in the winter and as a base for her beach vacations on the Côte d'Azur in the summer. As it turned out, she never stayed here in the summer and used the apartment only a few times in the winter, preferring to ski closer to home in Colorado. David and Elana came skiing with her one year when Nicole was about twelve years old. He would have loved to come more often, but his work never allowed it.

As they entered Valberg, he realized it might be the only town in France that had not changed one bit in the last ten years. He recognized every house even though he had only seen the town once before in the winter. He turned left toward the town of Péone and stopped in front of the Chalet de l'Alp. He knew the key would be under the doormat. His sister-in-law had told him how easy the arrangement with the real estate agent was. She just had to tell him that the apartment was rented and the agent would take care of everything else—clean the house, have the key under the mat, collect the money, restock towels and bedsheets as needed, and even make sure there was a basket of fruit on the counter when guests arrived.

Before they left Erdal and Yasemin, he took Erdal aside one more time and said, "You overheard my conversation with Nora's boss. Remember, you don't owe me anything. If you decide to take off before the two weeks are over, it's completely up to you. Clearly it is their preference that you wait here for two weeks and meet them. But I'm not telling you what your choice should be."

"But as my CIA handler you should tell me to call Langley, shouldn't you?"

"Yes, but I think we both have reasons to be suspicious of Langley's intentions at the moment. Clearly you were suspicious for the last five years."

"David...thank you."

After David and Nora left, Yasemin stared at Erdal.
"What?"

"Are you really willing to take the Israelis seriously?"

"I'm as suspicious of them as you are."

"Really? We are Turkish Muslims, and our kids have been going to Koran school on Saturdays. How do you think this works in Israel?"

"There are Arabs in Israel. And you have to admit, it would be the last place anyone would be looking for us."

"Please. It's one thing to move to Algeria where we'd fit in to some extent. But this?"

"I can see both sides of it. We have information that is valuable to the Israelis and they are willing to pay for it. On the other hand we'd end up living in circumstances that would feel even stranger than living in France. In Algeria, we'd be on our own but among people like us. I get it."

"Do you really? Then how do we settle this?"

"Not without some further digging. You heard David—he bought us two weeks. I think I will use the time to see what I can find."

"You plan to talk to Hani again?"

"I might."

"Be very careful. We still don't know whose side he is on. One more thing: Why is it two weeks? Did you tell David you needed two weeks?"

"No."

"So his schedule has something that happens within the next two weeks."

"He would have told me."

"Why would he?"

Erdal thought it over and had to admit Yasemin was right: there was no reason for David to offer an explanation unless he had to. So he asked himself a similar question that he over-heard on the phone earlier: What could possibly happen in these two weeks?

On the drive back, Nora was still testy. "What's next? You seem to have a two-week schedule. Can you fill me in on it?"

"There is no schedule. Erdal needs time to convince his family to make a move that seems quite radical to them."

"Seems to me his current situation is already radically different than the one he was in up until yesterday."

"It is. Which is precisely why the last thing he needs is more pressure. You heard Yasemin—she was about to crack."

Nora said nothing. She knew he had a point. But she still suspected David had an additional motive to buy time. As far as she was concerned, they had pretty much all the information they needed and should close the case.

After thinking about his next move for a while during the drive, David said: "I'll need to make a quick phone call to the US."

"I don't need to tell you it will be recorded and analyzed by certain friends of yours."

"Yes, I need to avoid key words that trigger their interest, and I need to mask my voice."

"You also need to pick carefully which number to call. Some receive more attention than others."

"I'm afraid I don't have that luxury." He rolled down the window to generate some background noise and dialed the phone number he had memorized after Bromberger's visit. Someone who sounded like she might be his secretary picked up.

He hoped she'd speak French and started by saying, "Could I leave a message for Monsieur Bromberger?"

"Certainly. What is the message? And could you speak up a little—there seems to be a lot of noise."

"If he is still interested in the property in Soldeu, our real estate agent in our Rue de Forbin office in Marseille could meet him on Wednesday morning. His name is Mamou Abderrahman."

"Soldeu property, Mamou Abderrahman can meet him Wednesday morning in his office in Marseille. He has the address?"

"Rue de Forbin."

"Right, you mentioned that. I will pass the message. If he has questions, how can he reach you?"

"At the office."

"Very well. Mr. Bromberger will be in touch."

"Merci beaucoup, madame."

Nora stared at him. "What was that?"

"I need someone's help to retrieve files from the CIA archives."

"And this person knows you as Mamou Abderrahman?"

"No, but he will pick up on a different keyword that will identify me. Mamou Abderrahman is the name of a café on the Rue de Forbin in Marseille. He will figure this part out—it is the only place to meet in that neighborhood."

"Not a professional then."

"Not one with established protocols—I had to make this one up."

"Not so bad as on-the-fly protocols go." She actually sounded impressed. "Hard to trace, sounded completely inconspicuous. Only one question: How far is Soldeu from where you normally stay?"

"Far enough to not be thrown into a search filter. Also enough of a tourist area to be credible."

"Yet you think he will recognize it as your key?"

"He introduced the location when I first met him."

Chapter 6

They arrived in Marseille on Tuesday afternoon and checked into the hotel La Joliette across the street from the Café Mamou Abderrahman. From the outside it looked like a little fleabag hotel in the middle of Marseille's Arab quarter. But the rooms were freshly renovated and clean. Most importantly, though, the window provided a perfect view of the café.

Next door they found a small brasserie that served specialties from the island of Corsica. David felt thrown back to his time as the station chief in Montpellier in the 1980s when he first found out about southern French cuisine, unpretentious red table wine, and the dry humor of the people who over many centuries figured out how to make a living in an area that had lots of rocks and little water, an area that was always neglected by whichever faraway government pretended to rule here. He felt the sudden urge to simply become one of them and vanish into this crowd that he had come to admire for its adaptability. But first he had a job to finish.

Nora asked: "How is your côte d'agneau?"

"Delicious. They seem to rub it in some interesting mix of herbs before they roast it."

"So what is your plan for tomorrow?"

"In the morning I will turn myself into a French country lawyer who is used to sipping his café au lait while reading the news and going through some paperwork at his local café before he wanders over to his office at the time we'd consider lunch hour. Nobody will think this is strange. All I need is a white shirt and a dark jacket from the bazaar down the street."

"I assume you'd like me to watch the street from the hotel window?"

"Yes, unless you prefer the brasserie right here."

"Hotel is better—nobody can see me there. Only problem is, how do we communicate?"

"I checked the windows. They can actually be opened. If there is real trouble and you're sure about it, drop the heavy glass vase that's on the desk in the room out the window followed by a loud French curse. If you're just suspicious about stuff, walk across the street to the brasserie and make sure I notice it—in this case, we'll have to improvise."

David entered the Café Mamou Abderrahman at 8:30 a.m. and found Bromberger already sitting at one of the tables in the back next to the bar. A quick survey of the other customers told him "all regulars." Normally he'd prefer to check more closely, but instead he sat down next to Bromberger. "Looks like you received my message."

"How can I help?"

"I need files."

"You are thinking of our little trespass into the archives?"

"You should start looking for a terror attack in a Minnesota shopping center. It will be exposed at the end of this week or early next. Once you find it, you will probably see similar records in the near vicinity. Take them all. Put them on a thumb drive. Do not store them on your hard drive to be copied to the thumb drive, but save them directly to the drive."

"Makes sense. How fast do you need this?"

"Faster is better."

"Tomorrow afternoon okay?"

David was stunned. He expected Bromberger to contact someone who did the work for him, fly back to the United States, and then come back to France, thumb drive in hand. "Does that mean you're doing it yourself?"

"Not everything. Someone in my office knows how to spin up a virtual machine image on some shady hosting service that we can hide behind. It's all temporary and gone without a trace after the work is done. All I have to do is log into the IP address he tells me and run some scripts to get things started. The searching is indeed my job, but I can do it from here."

"You know that most hosting services keep track of which account starts an image and where the account holder was logged in from?"

"Yes, but we are using someone else's account, and any log-in will use spoofed IP addresses that have been obtained from an anonymizer. If anybody were to look closely enough, it would appear that the hosting service is in a small African nation and has been controlled by a member of the Chinese military."

David knew this would sooner or later blow up and someone would get caught. He was glad he didn't have to do this work himself. For now he did believe that the cover would probably hold for a while, likely long enough for him. "When you have the drive ready, drop it at the hotel across the street for a 'Monsieur Baincroft.'"

"Is this your name while you are here?"

"No. But it will do the trick."

"Do you need anything else?"

David considered asking Bromberger for help with Erdal's family, but decided against it. Bromberger's operation seemed shaky at best, and when it collapsed, it would expose Erdal's next location. Instead, he said, "There is a chance I might have to fly someone out of the US without going through customs. Is this something you can help with?"

"I have access to a private jet that is parked at an airport where entry and exit are mostly governed by a self-declaration protocol. Your contact would show up for a shift as an airplane mechanic and someone else would take care of the checkout. When do you need this?"

"I don't know yet, but likely very soon. How much lead time do you need?"

"Probably a day."

They negotiated instructions for the passenger and a protocol for David to send a green-light message with a departure day. David was a little concerned about the requirement to call Bromberger's office repeatedly but could not think of a better way either without leaving his own number, which he knew would be a bad idea.

"One more thing. I know you are not used to secretive protocols and clandestine operations. It always sounds great when you read about it in books. But keep in mind what you risk. I can't teach you want you need to know in a few hours here in a café. But you'll have to remember a few things. Most importantly, you cannot talk to anybody. Not your wife, not your kids, not your business associates, not even your board—maybe one day to your grandkids, but not now. Second, if you think nobody is watching you, that's because of your lack of attention. Start looking for who is watching you and think of a way to evade them. There is nothing wrong with being paranoid—they really are after you. Third, assume every step you take is monitored in some way."

Bromberger thought about it and knew he had already violated at least two out of three. He was hoping things would move quickly enough that precautions became irrelevant. He said, "I'll keep it in mind."

"Oh, and one more thing: things never move as quickly as you think and the outcome will never be what your best-case-scenario says."

Looking at Bromberger, David knew he had guessed his thoughts correctly. *Typical amateur.*

The unexpected time line in recovering the files he needed, although welcome news, presented David with a dilemma. His next call with Henry and James was scheduled for Friday morning. Getting back to his Pyrenean hideout would be close to impossible without a car. He did not want to leave Nora in charge of the pickup given the sensitivity of the material. He thought about asking to reschedule for Monday morning but figured it would raise unnecessary suspicions.

When he looked around the hotel room, he figured there might be a different solution. There were just two things he needed. He sketched one of them on a piece of paper and asked Nora to see if she could find a similar lamp in a furniture store. Then he asked the concierge for the nearest Apple store and was surprised to learn he'd have to travel either to Aix-en-Provence or Montpellier. He settled instead for "Le Mac d'Occasion," which sold used Macintosh computers just south of the train station. He was wondering for a moment whether Marseille was the last city in the civilized world without an Apple store.

"Can you tell me why you need this ugly lamp?"

"Because it's just as ugly as the one that sits behind me in all my videoconferences and I need to rig this room to look just like my home office from the camera angle."

"And you think that will work?"

"I can hope, can't I?"

"If they see this every week, a tiny bit of different wall color or a shadow that wasn't there before will tip them off. Even the audio having unusual background noise will cause suspicion."

"They have no reason to be suspicious." He knew better than that, but was hoping. He also hadn't thought of the background noise problem—after all this was a hotel in a busy street with traffic, not a mountain cabin.

"Weren't you gone for two weeks?"

"Yes, but they don't know that."

"You're sure?"

Of course he wasn't, but he was willing to risk it. So he prepared his used laptop to tunnel into his network using the backdoor he had left open before starting his travels. He checked his log files to see if James's monitoring showed any unusual activity. There was only a slight deviation from the normal routine: normally, the daily activity logs for the network would be transferred at midnight and crunched into summary reports for the next morning. On Tuesday, this happened twice—at noon and again at midnight. Someone had requested a manual snapshot.

He tweaked the settings on his router to redirect incoming video requests through the VPN tunnel to the video of his new laptop and tested the picture briefly to make sure the angle worked and the image would resemble his usual home office closely enough. Nora was right; he had enough reason to be worried. But right now, he had no choice.

As David was walking through the lobby, the front desk manager stopped him.

"Ah, Monsieur Baincroft."

"Oui."

"Somebody just dropped off this envelope for you."

"Thank you."

He opened the padded envelope and found the thumb drive as he had expected. He also found a handwritten note: "Cannot accommodate transport request. Sorry."

David wondered why Bromberger was not able to help, but did not have time to think about it. He wanted to check the files as quickly as possible.

As he was going through the files, he noticed that Yuri's prediction was accurate. Apparently, four young men of Pakistani origin had been spoon-fed ideas for a terror plot in Bloomington, Minnesota. They would leave a large SUV filled to the roof with explosives in a parking garage under the Mall of America where it would inflict maximum damage if it exploded. Except it would not explode since all the material sold to them came from a source the ringleader had suggested. It was packaged the same way military-grade explosives are, mostly to look good on camera. But the C4 was really just recycled plastic. Police would pick up the four kids in the early morning hours on Tuesday, just after they placed the vehicle in the parking lot.

David knew his next step would be risky to the point of being irresponsible. But he could not just sit there and do nothing. He created a fresh account at torproject.org using a spoofed IP address that he knew would be traceable to a US secret service network section. He suspected his agency friends were monitoring all new account requests at Tor and considered this his little private joke on them. He then used the anonymized session to send an e-mail to a reporter he had run into in the past, using a Gmail account he created solely for this purpose only to delete it right after he was done. After that he closed his Tor account and logged off. He knew well enough that the reporter would not be able to do anything with the information right now. But he hoped that by next Tuesday, she might remember having seen the exact same plot outlined before it happened in an e-mail that she had discarded as completely outrageous and impossible.

NEXT MORNING. SAINT PAUL, MINNESOTA.

Judith Ingersson had been covering national security for her local Minneapolis paper and other regional and national papers for many years—occasionally, even the *New York Times* picked up her work. Part of the job was to be able to weed through an unbelievable amount of e-mails from conspiracy theorists all over the country asking her how she could have possibly missed this or that totally obvious detail. Among her favorites were mails like "9/11 Terrorists TRAINED BY CIA", "Saddam Hussein Alive - Seen In Colorado Springs Supermarket" or "Obama in Cahoots With Saudi Intelligence to Drive Up Price of Gas". By now she was able to recognize them by simply looking at the subject lines. She never even checked the content before pressing the delete button.

This morning she went through her regular routine when one e-mail subject made her stop. It read, "Don't Delete: Bombing Plot Will Be Discovered in Three Days."

The use of future tense was unusual. All her regular customers were focusing on past events. She read through the first paragraph where the e-mail talked about a terror plot to be uncovered within the next few days. It mentioned a group of four young Pakistani men by name and predicted they'd be arrested at a specific time in the morning. It also predicted the exact make and model of the car they were planning to use for a bomb and the license plate.

Judith was amused. *That's a completely new level of crackpot.* She decided she'd keep the e-mail for three days and see if anything would happen. Then her day became busy and she forgot everything about the mail.

LA JOLIETTE HOTEL, MARSEILLE.

Nora showed no signs of leaving the room for David's talk with Henry and James. He was getting anxious about it, not sure how to approach the topic with her. Nora finally smiled at him and said, "I'll get some coffee across the street. Should I bring some back for you?"

"Thanks, that would be great."

"About an hour?"

"Probably less, but an hour should be fine."

"Why do men never know how to ask for things?"

"What?"

"You were getting more and more nervous as the time for your call approached. I finally guessed that you were not that comfortable with me around. But men never find the words, do they?"

"Or maybe we concentrate on the important stuff."

"Like what? No, don't answer that."

Nora had just left the room when his videoconference invite sounded. James left the conversation to Henry, who was in no hurry to get started with the reason he was on the call.

"How was the Tour?"

Crap. He completely forgot to read up on what happened at the stage he supposedly watched. "It was great. I keep forgetting how grueling these mountain stages are. Everybody looks like they lost half their weight by the time they arrive at the top."

"Did you see the crash?"

"Which one? There were at least two on the day I was there but I was higher up."

"I read somewhere they had a real big pileup that knocked out some of the favorites."

"Yup, crashing the bike still kills more careers than doping convictions." He hoped the slight chuckle he got out of this comment would help dodge the conversation about race results and was relieved to hear Henry move off the topic.

However, the topic he was getting to wasn't much better.

"Remember, when you transferred to the SigInt group, you kept handling a field agent who refused to accept anyone else as his contact?"

"Yes, our high-profile al-Qaeda man." He chose not to mention the fact that it was the same group that was widely blamed for his assassination attempt.

"We need to find him."

"After five years of radio silence? Am I missing something?"

"We probably should have asked you to help earlier but we had a few promising leads from other agencies. But now it seems that it all has run dry."

"Assuming we can find him, what is the plan?"

"We need to question him about the other members of the group."

"Since he was always pretty clear about how he works, what makes you think he would cooperate?"

"Cooperation is not required in this case."

"Meaning he'd be going to one of our torture camps for questioning?"

"We don't have torture camps."

"Right, new president says we don't torture anymore. So is it 'interrogation camp outside US jurisdiction' or some euphemism like that?"

"Come on, David. I thought we were on the same side."

David thought about what he had just seen in the files he received from Bromberger, and he was not so sure which side he should be on. "You know which side I'm on—I would never hesitate when it comes to saving American lives. But I need to know what's going on, if you want me to be effective."

"The main thing you need to know is that we need to bring your man in."

"So what makes this urgent enough to bring me out of hiding and run the risk of my being alive becoming known?"

"We think the group is reconfiguring and planning new work."

"And what do you have for me to start with since this is a five-year-old cold case?"

"We have prepared a file with all the information we could get from fellow agencies, law enforcement, and other sources. It's not a lot, but you have access to all of it—plus all your old material. Take a look around, familiarize yourself, then let's talk on Monday."

"Sounds like a plan." It wasn't a plan he liked, but he'd have to play along.

"One more thing. We have sent you a technician to upgrade your equipment for the latest encryption standards and to make sure you have all the proper access."

"When?"

"She should be there by early afternoon. She is expected to land in Toulouse this morning."

David walked to the café as soon as his call ended. "Nora, I need your help."

"You look like crap. What's going on?"

"Please rent a car. I will pack. I will explain as soon as we are on the road."

Nora just nodded and walked out.

David started packing their luggage and checked out of the hotel. He collected the bicycles and took the front wheels off hoping to fit them into the trunk of whatever car Nora would come back with. If this wouldn't work, they'd have to leave them behind.

It took Nora only half an hour to come back to the hotel. She had a Peugeot station wagon, which held the bikes and the luggage without any problem.

"So what is going on now? I take it your call did not go quite as planned?"

It took David a moment before he could answer. He decided there was no point holding back much information since they'd be forced to work together, if he wanted to have any chance of success.

"The agency suspects that Erdal is trying to set up his old terror network again and they want me to find him and bring him in."

"At least it's an easy job."

He shot her an angry look.

"Sorry. I should listen first, I guess."

"They made it pretty clear that he is supposed to be brought into what they now call 'severe interrogation detention.' It means they consider him hostile and have no problem burning him."

"I assume you are pretty certain that he is not hostile?"

"We have worked together for more than twenty years. I think I'd know."

"Just asking since I wouldn't know and I'm naturally suspicious. Plus, when we met him, he gave no indication which side he was on."

"He did when he and I talked. Also, we now know that there never was any real terror cell—only a conference of representatives of all major agencies. So an attempt to bring it back together seems pretty ridiculous."

Nora frowned and said, "I think that's precisely what's happening."

"You're losing me."

"Don't you get it? If your people are lying to you, they probably will use some version that is pretty close to the truth. What if Erdal was following the same thoughts we did for the last two weeks? What if he started his own digging efforts and reconnected to some of his old contacts? He may not know it, but he just pushed a stick into a hornet's nest since everybody he could possibly talk to is part of some agency that has contacts to yours. He's the only one left without the inside scoop."

"So you're saying they are not worried about him having gone rogue, but about him finding out about the real purpose of the old cell."

"Yes. And they think you are the only one he would trust enough so that he would not run immediately."

"Sounds totally crazy. But unfortunately, I think you might be right."

"So do you really think it's wrong to bring him in?"

David realized it was time to disclose at least some of the information he found on Bromberger's memory stick. "I have not told you about the results from my meeting yesterday yet. I received a copy of the internal CIA files of an operation known as the Anderssen Gambit. It is based on—"

"A nineteenth-century chess player who trapped his opponents by sacrificing strategically important pieces."

"Yes. I wrote the original paper on it that analyzed the FSB activities. The paper was called the Anderssen Gambit after the strategic patterns we found in the FSB's activities. It then was taken further by a faction inside the agency that proposed the CIA should learn from the Russians and apply similar techniques. At the time, most people were appalled by the suggestion, and I thought that was the end of it.

"But apparently they found covert funding and not only started the program, but connected to other groups with a similar mind-set in agencies in friendly nations and even in competing nations like Russia and China. None of this goes to any official level, but it is run by factions of ambitious agents who have a completely novel idea of the purpose of a secret service. This is the main reason why we see so many easily uncovered terror plots in recent years."

"So you are telling me that they are really all manufactured? I'm still not buying it."

"On Tuesday, the police in Bloomington, Minnesota, will find a car bomb ready to explode in the underground parking lot of a local shopping mall. The vehicle is a Toyota Highlander, and it will have military-grade explosives that can be linked to groups in Afghanistan."

"This upcoming Tuesday?"

"Yes. The police will arrest four young men of Pakistani origin that have been living in the US for over fifteen years. Nothing will be disclosed about how they were found. The truth is that it was a group of five and the real ringleader who procured the explosives, came up with the plan, stole the car, and recruited the four members is a CIA agent."

"But they were still going along with the plan. So it's not like they are innocent bystanders."

"Yes, very likely they targeted a group of young males who are dissatisfied with their lives and were talking about how they wish they could do something about it. In a normal world, it would have all remained just talk. If every time during my teenage years someone had been ready to help me implement one of my crazy ideas born out of frustration, I would have spent my life in jail."

"Okay, but how many of these plots are real and how many are the type you just described?"

"Very few are real. September 11 was real. The Madrid train bombings were real. And the attack on the embassy in Benghazi. Not much else is. I have a complete list of things that the agency directly instigated."

"What are you going to do about it?"

"I'm not sure yet."

"You know, where I work, we deal with real problems; we don't need to manufacture additional ones. We can always use some help from people who know what they are doing."

"Nice pitch. Is that part of your mission, to make sure you recruit me?"

Nora was silent for a while then said, "Yes. But it wasn't supposed to go like this. This is becoming much bigger than any of us thought."

"Tell your boss I'm not ready to defect. I think the agency can be fixed, and I'm not ready to give up. But I'm willing to engage in a tentative alliance that helps both of us."

"You'll become a double agent then."

"No. We will consult and decide on a case-by-case basis how much information we are willing to share."

"He will not like that."

"I know."

"You have not told me yet what created the urgency to drive immediately. Neither where we are going."

"Sorry. Part of my reactivation is that they have sent someone to upgrade my network so that I can get access to what I need inside the agency."

"And where is this person right now?

"Toulouse."

"Going to Barcelona?"

"Closer to Andorra."

"Shouldn't we drive faster then?"

"Yes. Also, one more problem."

"Oh?"

"I was hoping to enlist someone's help to fly my daughter out of the US without being noticed by US customs. But the plan has fallen apart."

"If you're asking me for help, any such extraction would take a few weeks of preparation."

"I know. I am leaning toward a simpler plan. But it would require someone to pick her up in Paris and avoid any tails."

"Which is where you think I come in."

"Yes, there is a pickup location in Paris that I can instruct her to get to. But she would need help avoiding detection after that—clearing her electronic trail, replacing credit cards, avoiding registration in any hotels, all that stuff."

"How will you get her there?"

"She is close to the Canadian border, and driving north is nothing unusual for events like a concert, so it won't raise any serious suspicions. Then she can just drive herself to the airport and book a flight when she walks in. By the time it raises a flag, she has landed in Paris and is off with you."

"All correct as long as you can be sure that she is not on their radar yet. But the moment this happens, they know she's evading them."

"Not necessarily. She can post on her Facebook page that she decided on a whim to go to Europe for a week. It will help—she's twenty-three years old. This should be normal behavior."

"Not for someone in witness protection."

"Everybody gets sick of things at one point. And I'm hoping she doesn't need a lot of lead time."

"How will you get a message to her?"

"We use an anonymous chat server."

"Truly anonymous?"

"As good as I was able to set up."

"I might have a better way."

David looked at her puzzled.

"What? I tried to become her friend for a year, so I know a few things about her."

"Like what?"

"For example that she still speaks to her ex-boyfriend. And that I can get a message to him to pass on without raising suspicions."

"She has a boyfriend?"

"Someone should really teach a class for aspiring fathers. The fact that nobody knows how to speak to their daughters is pathetic."

David decided not to take the bait. "Why do you think this is a good channel?"

"He's one of us."

"Oh great."

"Whatever. You of all people should know how covert operations work."

"Doesn't mean I have to like the fact that my family has become the target of one."

"It comes in handy right now. So how do you tell her about the meeting place?"

When Nicole was eight years old they had spent a week in Paris. The evening they arrived, they had dinner at l'Ilot Vache, an expensive restaurant on the Cité. Nicole didn't like the food much but instantly fell in love with the double chocolate mousse on the dessert menu. Every night during the trip she asked whether they could go back to the "Moose Café" and drew pictures of a moose everywhere she could find a scrap of paper. Even years later they were still telling the story and laughing about the Moose Café. Asking her to meet him there would be incomprehensible to anyone outside his family, but Nicole would immediately understand it as his message with precise coordinates coming from an authenticated sender.

"We have a natural code name for a meeting place in Paris."

"And you would tell her to expect me?"

"No need. She knows you, right?"

"Yes."

Something about the answer seemed a little too tentative. "What's wrong?"

"I'm not sure if she will talk to me, if she expects you."

"I don't understand."

"Look, we didn't necessarily get along too well."

David started to get exasperated. As if working with an inexperienced agent wasn't enough, now he had to deal with teenage animosity on top of it. This was definitely not what he wanted to hear.

"Since I don't know what the problem is between you two, does this mean you are not able to do this, or will you find a way?"

"I always find a way."

He was still plagued by doubts but kept his mouth shut.

Back at his cabin, David went through everything to make sure it had remained undisturbed during his absence. He checked all the network logs to see if there was anything unusual, but found no evidence of anything being different while he was gone. He then had to turn off all his "toys" to avoid them being detected during the maintenance upgrade, and he was just done when his visitor arrived.

"Angela! I'm surprised they sent you."

"Good or bad surprise?"

"Always good." Angela had been on his team in the SigInt group he had run. They had the start of an office fling a few months before the attack. It never became serious, but Henry knew about it and had personally intervened to shut them down. David still remembered a very uncomfortable visit to Henry's office behind closed doors. The fact that he sent Angela meant that this was not a regular technology upgrade—it was a checkup on David.

Angela was done with the technology portion of her work in less than an hour.

"So they fly you to this place in the middle of nowhere so that you can do a one-hour job that could be done just the same in a remote ssh session?"

"David, how long have you been working for the agency? You should know better. Of course I need to take you through the activation script."

Angela took him through a subset of the probing questions they would normally subject a new agent to. They spent hours talking about seemingly irrelevant topics. But David knew better than to evade any subjects and show boredom or irritability. Instead, he patiently answered questions about his state of mind, whether he had talked to people from his past, why not, how much he kept informed on the news, what he thought about aspects of his life in the mountains, and many more seemingly irrelevant topics. By 6:00 p.m. David felt like he had just come back from the world's most exhausting workout. Actually, this was precisely what it was called: "the workout."

He said, "Had Henry announced you a little earlier, I could have made you dinner. But as things stand, I think we'll have to go to the local pub. Don't expect anything fancy."

They arrived at La Pobla just after eight and caused the few locals in the bar to turn heads as they walked in. This was not the place where crowds of tourists showed up.

"I take it you don't come here regularly?"

"I've been here maybe two or three times total."

"So what do you do then?"

"Make my own dinner, read, grow vegetables, make wine, hike through the mountains, talk to James." He rolled his eyes with the last comment, which caused her to laugh.

"He's quite the pain in the rear, isn't he?"

"It's his job. But yes, he is."

"It is five years since your wife and daughter died, right?" David had not realized that the story told inside the agency might be different from person to person. Clearly Angela did not know that he and Nicole were in the car together after the attack.

"Yes, and the pain has not gotten any better, if that's what you meant to ask."

"I know. My sister lost her husband and son in a car accident. A year later she killed herself. I can only imagine what it's like being stuck alone in the mountains with this weighing on you."

"I can't pretend it has been easy."

"Any thoughts of revenge?" David was wondering whether this was still part of the checkup, and he guessed that it was.

"I would not know who the revenge should target. I don't think we really know who was behind this. But if I'd face this person tomorrow, I'm not sure what I would do."

"Not that I know what the real story was, aside from what we all heard in the news. But I heard rumors that you led an operative who was planted deep in an al-Qaeda cell, which found out about the connection and tried to eliminate you. Is any of that true?"

"The fact that we successfully infiltrated a cell, yes. Everything else is conjecture as far as I know."

"It's been five years—has anybody looked into this?"

"I haven't been allowed near anything for the last five years, so I'd be literally the last to know. But it seems that my reactivation might lead me into related territory. But since you're here, you probably already know."

"Not really. All I knew was that your hardware required checking and same for your state of mind. Tomorrow I'll be on my way back. Speaking of which, do you have space in your cabin or do I have to find a hotel?"

"I can guarantee that you will not find a hotel unless you are willing to drive for a long time. Yes, I can make space for you."

She grabbed his hand and said, "It's been five years. And things have changed, haven't they?"

"Yes, they have." David knew exactly what Angela meant and had to admit after five years of solitary life he was starved for affection. "The cabin is under full video surveillance."

"We might have to cut a circuit or two."

David smiled. He always liked the fact that Angela had a bit of a mischievous streak.

Chapter 7

"So how did your meeting with David go?"

"Upgrade is finished, and he has access to everything he needs."

"Angela, that wasn't what I meant."

"He is fine. Surprisingly stable after what he has gone through. I think you can cut him some slack. But you were right—he does know how to mess with the video signal and probably other things as well."

"I would have been surprised if he didn't. He was always our go-to person for intrusions."

"I think he enjoys it mostly for his personal amusement and to keep himself sharp."

"How can you be sure?"

Angela thought for a minute and had to admit she couldn't know for sure. But her official answer: "He made no attempt to hide any of it. Quite the contrary, he seemed to have almost a prankster's pride in how he can toy with whatever we set up for him."

"Okay, for now I'll take your word for it. What has he been up to?"

"He has made the place into some sort of organic self-sufficient farm. He showed me his whole production and was really proud of it. You should try his vegetable omelet, if you ever get the chance. I think he started to enjoy his life as Pablo the farmer and seemed almost sorry to leave it behind. He even makes decent red wine from the grapes he grows up there."

"Any signs of visitors or him doing stuff he shouldn't?"

"He told me he had a single visitor all these years and it scared him almost to death. Some German dude who got lost on his bike, looking for Andorra."

"A few weeks ago?"

"Yes, that's what he said."

"Right afterward he left to watch the Tour."

"Yup, he's a bit of a biking nut. He secretly keeps a travel bike, and he thinks you don't know about it."

"I was wondering how he got around since no record of him obtaining transport showed up on our radar."

"He knew that should raise suspicions. He wanted to find out how closely you are monitoring him. I think he was a little disappointed that you didn't even ask."

"What else have you been talking about?"

"It's all in my report. I finished it on the flight back."

"No, I mean the stuff that's not in the report."

"Oh, just old times."

"As in good old times?"

"Yes. And that's as much as I'll say since everything else really is irrelevant."

Henry was wondering whether he made the right decision to send Angela to check on David. He also knew he had to go with what he knew now and decided to move forward. But first he would check on the German tourist.

SUNDAY MORNING. LANGLEY.

"James, can you pull up those videos from the surprise visitor David had a few weeks ago?"

"We had gone through them already, right?"

"Can you pull them up?"

"One second... On screen now."

"Have they been tampered with in any way?"

"That would be completely impossible. They are stored on a secure encrypted drive and are accessible only to accounts with the proper credentials."

"You have not answered my question."

"I will have to take a much closer look and it will take me a while. But there is no obvious sign. What are you suspecting?"

"How would we know if some of the content had been deleted?"

"We'd see evidence of splicing—uneven transitions, sudden difference in lighting, gaps in the audio, stuff like that."

"And you have checked that?"

"No, there was no need."

"There is a need now."

"It will take me a few hours."

"Few hours? Jeeze. Okay, so let's take a look at them in the meantime."

They were watching as David's doorbell rang and someone in sweaty biking clothes showed up speaking in heavily accented Spanish, then switching to French, later to German. "What the hell are they talking about?"

"I think they are trying to negotiate which language they are both most comfortable with."

"And what's the result?"

"Appears to be German. I took it in high school, and it seems like David first tried to brush him off, but then he took pity on him because the guy had to be in Andorra the next morning and there is nothing else in between."

"I thought there was some ski resort close by?"

"Yes, but that's toward France, not Andorra."

They watched the conversation over dinner for a while as Bromberger spoke about his bike trip.

"What's this now?"

"As far as I can tell he is talking about a bike trip, probably how he got there and got lost. But there are a lot of words I never heard before."

"I knew David was fluent in French and Spanish. Does he know German as well?"

"His first assignment was as a liaison to a military outfit in Illesheim, Germany."

"What are they talking about now?"

"I'm afraid I don't understand a single word."

"They switched languages again?"

"I'm not sure."

"Go back and find out."

James went back a few minutes to find out what happened. "Seems like here is the switch. David's asking whether he's from Nuremburg. And then without any notice, they both speak some totally weird stuff—it does not sound like German at all, but I have no idea what it is."

"Any relation to Arabic or Slavic languages?"

"None that I could tell. I speak enough Russian and would be able to pick that up. And Arabic we hear all the time here—it has a totally different cadence."

"Couldn't be Chinese or something, right?"

"Not that I'm the expert, but none of them even looks Chinese."

Henry looked out the window. It was a bright day with clear skies, yet it felt to him like a fierce thunderstorm was moving in. If David and his visitor were actively hiding the content of their conversation, it meant something very bad was going on. "How do we find out what this is?"

"I will get one of our linguistics experts to take a look."

"Find out what language this is and get me someone who can translate it. Quickly."

James didn't like having to create a weekend emergency for the linguistics department. There was very little that justified getting the translators and language analytics people to work on a Sunday, but he figured he'd better have an answer for Henry by the end of the day. He called a friend who deemed himself an expert in "dying languages" and asked him to listen to the audio portion to identify the language. To his surprise, he had an answer within thirty minutes.

"Ah, the unofficial language of the court of Charlemagne. How did you come across this?"

"What on earth are you talking about?"

"In the empire of the Franks, the official language of the court was high Latin. But the commoners spoke their own language known today as 'Alt Frankish.' Traces of it can still be found in France, Luxembourg, in areas along the river Moselle, and most prominently in northern Bavaria in a region known to this day as 'Franken.' That's where your customers are from."

"Are you serious? Where the hell is that?"

"Largest city is Nuremburg—remember, where we held the trials after World War II?"

It started to make sense to James. "Do we have any military installations there?"

"Quite a few actually. There is a tank division in Illesheim, and some tactical nuclear weapons are deployed nearby. Are you worried someone might attack them?"

"No, this relates to a totally different geography, which is why we were caught off guard by the use of this language —'Frankish,' you said?"

"Yes."

"Does anybody in your group know how to translate it?"

"The person who identified it has worked in Bamberg in the past. She says she understands most of it and will e-mail you a transcript later tonight. By the way, she thinks one of them speaks it with an American accent."

When he looked at the transcript later in the evening, James thought Henry had clearly overreacted. There was talk about bicycles, mountain passes, directions to Andorra, and lots of talk about food and how to prepare it. Nothing at all that could possibly be suspicious. The translator had only a single annotation where she wasn't sure about the meaning. It read ,"I'm not sure about the use of the word 'shdaahbillds.' I first couldn't make much sense of it, but now I suspect it refers to some mushroom variety, possibly porcini, and I translated it accordingly." He forwarded the e-mail to Henry and went to sleep thinking, *I really hate weekend fire drills*.

David had spent the weekend looking through the material Henry wanted him to read and the files he received from Bromberger. Henry's material was a subsection. Most files existed in multiple variants that were prepared for different audiences. David knew this was standard procedure since people with different security clearance would have to be given access to the same files, but were not allowed to see the whole document. In the old days, regions would simply be blackened on paper. Now the CIA used a document management system where branches of the same document could be maintained independently. This way a public disclosure request would produce one type of document that had been stripped of any information the agency deemed necessary to be kept secret, whereas an agent with proper clearance would always see the original copy of the document (or any derivative he or she was interested in).

Usually this technique was used to keep selective details secret, but the general drift of the document would always remain intact. In this case, it was totally different. None of the details had been kept hidden from him. But the interpretation and analysis were completely reversed. He was being set up to believe a story that was known inside the agency to be a fraud. He did not sleep well that night.

MONDAY MORNING. SYRACUSE, NEW YORK.

Erica was late for a meeting with Dr. Chen, her lab supervisor. She had come home late from that strange party last night. Where the hell did she park her car? That's when she saw Josh waiting for her.

"I'm in a hurry. What do you want?"

"I have a message."

Josh did not usually talk like this. Something in his tone of voice made her stop. "What kind of message?"

"Wait, I had to write it down—to make sure I get it right."

She looked at the piece of paper Josh had handed to her and suddenly felt dizzy. "How do you know about the Moose Café?"

"I don't, which is why I had to write it down. Does this make any sense to you?"

She wanted to ask how he knew her father but thought better of it. Instead, she simply said, "Yes."

"Then I have more instructions. We can walk while I tell you."

"My car is right here, hop in."

"Wherever this café is, you are expected there tomorrow at lunch, local time. This part is important: drive across the border to Canada and leave from there. If your passport is scanned at the border, the border guard will see a message on his computer screen and he will ask you where you are going and when you expect to be back. Tell them you are going to Toronto for the White Stripes concert and that you are staying with friends for a week."

"I can't stand the White Stripes."

"You need to concentrate right now. I know you have a crisis in the lab and are due for a paper. I will help with Chen and will ask Professor Roberts for an extension. You can deal with all this when you get back. One more thing: when you get to Canada, update your Facebook page to tell everybody you ran into friends from Switzerland and are joining them for a week or two in the mountains."

"I don't have friends in Switzerland."

"I know."

"Josh, what's going on?" She had to suppress the tears in her eyes.

"I have no idea. I'm only the messenger."

She felt the ground shifting under her—clearly Josh was not who she thought he was. "I am scared. Who are you really?"

"It's better, if you don't know."

"What we had—was any of it real?"

"I'm trying to help. You need to leave. Let me out here, then hurry. One more thing: be very careful."

While she was packing her bags, she thought about the message she had just received. Only two people in the world knew about the restaurant in Paris that she had called "Moose Café" when she was a little kid. Her mother was dead, so this message could only come from her father. Why had he not used their regular chat session? He must think it had been compromised. He did not want her to travel from a US airport. So he was worried about the US government looking for her. But what was Josh's role? He had been her boyfriend, and she thought they were still friends. Now it turns out he was somehow connected to her father? Creepy.

She packed light, checked online—there was indeed a concert of the Stripes in Toronto the same night, so she bought a ticket online figuring it might make her story more credible. Her witness protection status meant she was supposed to check in with the marshal's office before she left for a trip, especially when she left the country. But she had not talked to them in ages and figured there was no need.

She packed her cell phone and considered taking her laptop but decided against it—she could always update her Facebook page from some public terminal in an Internet café. Then she was ready to leave.

David's talk with Henry was shorter than expected. Henry seemed barely interested in David's thoughts or plans. They agreed that David should travel to meet some old contacts and that he could use his current identity as Pablo Poixtras when he needed to cross borders or show his identity. *This was much too easy*.

Despite the newfound latitude, David still wanted to make sure he could limit being tracked. He had no intention of letting Henry know where he was at all times. He started packing his travel bags, including his official phone, his agency-issued secure laptop, his collection of burner phones, and the memory stick he had received from Bromberger. Then he walked to the grocery store in town to ask Jose where to rent a car.

"All these years, you travel by bike and now you need a car? Gotten lazy with age?"

Normally he enjoyed Jose's teasing, but today David was a bit impatient. "Not lazy, busy."

Jose raised an eyebrow. People didn't suddenly get busy around here, but he liked Pablo and wasn't going to give him a hard time. "My son is actually driving down to Girona later to get supplies and talk to our insurance agent. I'm sure he won't mind giving you a ride. Girona is tourist-central. You will find plenty of rental car places there."

"Thank you. When do I need to be ready?"

"Alejandro, when do you want to leave?"

"As soon as I'm done stacking these cases down here in the basement."

Jose turned to the back and looked down the staircase, then determined, "Be ready in an hour."

David went back to his cabin, took one more look around to make sure nothing important was left behind, then grabbed his bags to walk out. He did not expect to return.

TUESDAY MORNING. PARIS - CHARLES DE GAULLE.

Erica van Wyden walked through customs at Charles de Gaulle airport without any trouble. She looked for a cell phone store, found one in the arrival hall, and bought a prepaid SIM card for her phone. She put the card into the empty slot where she had removed her regular SIM card at home. Then she opened Google Maps to look for restaurants on the Ile de la Cité and entered "vache" as the search term since she remembered dimly that the logo of the restaurant she was looking for had a cow's head in it. Only one match: l'Ilot Vache, not really on the Cité, but on the neighboring Ile Saint-Louis. The RER train from the airport would take her to the Les Halles station from where she could either walk or take the metro for one more stop.

It was a nice day and she decided to walk across the bridge from Les Halles. Coming out of the RER station, she saw the Centre Pompidou and passed it to walk toward town hall—she had always wondered why the French insisted on calling it the "the town's hotel." She walked another block to the river where she had a magnificent view of Notre Dame and she could see the Eiffel Tower farther back. Another short walk along the river would take her to the Ile Saint-Louis. She had been to Paris only twice in her life, once with her parents many years ago and then for a school trip with her French class. Even though she had nothing but fond memories of the city, it now made her feel very uncomfortable. Clearly her father had some serious concern or he would not have come up with this awkward meeting routine.

She arrived at the Pont Marie and turned right onto the small island in the middle of the river Seine. She knew from Google Maps to look on her right for the restaurant that was the designated meeting point with her father; she found it after another five minutes. She sat down at a table next to the window facing the street.

Nora had watched from across the street as Nicole walked to the Ilot Vache. She continued to watch the street for another ten minutes to make sure nobody else was interested in her arrival. Finally satisfied, she walked into the restaurant to join at the same table.

"Hello, Nicole."

It finally dawned on Nicole that this was nothing but a cruel practical joke played by this idiotic chick Sara Baur and her ex-boyfriend Josh. Fighting the tears, she left some euros for the coffee she just had, got up, and grabbed her backpack to go back to the airport and fly home.

"Sit down, Nicole. Aren't you wondering how I know your real name? Or why your father sent me to pick you up?"

Nicole looked at the person she knew as Sara and decided to listen to her story.

"Thank you. Do you have your cell phone with you?"

Nicole took her phone out of her pocket and put it on the table. Nora grabbed it, took the battery out, and checked the SIM card. "Prepaid?"

"Yes. Why?"

"Because it won't help. Here is your new phone. Please wait, I'll be right back."

Nicole watched confused as Nora left the restaurant and was looking for one of the street kids she had seen earlier. She found a group of them around the corner.

"Hey, I have a phone you might be interested in."

One of the teenagers came closer, looked at the phone and asked, "Combien?" ("How much?")

"It's free. There is even a card in it. Just promise me you'll make a few phone calls with it during the day."

The kid looked at her suspiciously. "Is this some sort of trick? Are you with the flics?"

"No trick, and do I really look like a cop?"

When she got back to the restaurant, Nicole had organized her thoughts.

"What is going on here?" she demanded.

"Fair question. But if you don't mind, let's not discuss in a public place like this. I need to fill you in on a lot of things, and we need to get out of Paris. We have a long drive, so you can ask me tons of questions."

"I'm not going anywhere until I know what's going on. And a public place suits me just fine."

Nora looked around. It was Monday close to lunch hour and the place was still almost empty, but it would be filled very soon.

"Okay, listen. My name is Nora Weizmann, not Sara Baur. I am not a student. I was at Syracuse to watch you, hoping you might be connected to your father and lead me to him. We found him through a different connection, and I have been working with him for the last two weeks. He was not able to come himself and asked me to meet you here."

Nicole thought about what Nora said. She didn't know exactly what kind of work her father did, but knew it was dangerous. She had her own taste of it when their house was blown up, which was likely intended to kill them all—this was indeed what her witness protection officer had always pointed out to her—even though he thought the bomb was set by some drug lord. But all she knew about Nora was that she was watching her secretly, which was already creepy, and she had never liked her to begin with. So at a minimum she needed confirmation that this was not a trap.

"If everything is as you say, you must have a way to contact my father."

"I do."

"Call him. Now."

Nora hesitated, then took out a phone, and dialed one of David's burner phones. She hoped that he would have kept it on. After seven rings, David finally picked up. Before Nora was able to say anything, Nicole snatched the phone with a quick move Nora would have not guessed she was capable of.

"Who is this?"

"Nicole? Oh my god, it's so good to finally hear your voice again."

"Dad—this woman wants me to come with her to meet you."

"Please trust me on this and do exactly what she asks you to do. She is a friend and she will help. We have to hurry a little. I'd love to talk more, but I will see you soon. I love you, Nicole. Please let me talk to Nora quickly."

When Nora took back the phone she noticed that it was wet and Nicole was sobbing relentlessly. She put a hand on her arm while taking the phone with the other. "David, we are still in Paris. Are we still meeting you on Thursday?"

"The timing might shift a little. I am driving to meet some people. I will let you know."

"So your meeting yesterday went well, I take it?"

"Hard to say. It was strange."

"Okay, so for now I will stick to the plan until I hear from you."

"Thank you for doing this."

"Not a problem. Just don't create any trouble."

Nora helped Nicole pack the backpack into the trunk of the Peugeot she had rented in Marseille. She decided to give her passenger some time before dumping a ton of information on her. But Nicole wanted to get right to the point.

"So who exactly are you working for?"

"It's a long story but we have a few hours. You are Jewish, right?"

"I don't know. My mother was, I guess that means I am, too."

"Do you know how the state of Israel was founded?"

"Sort of—we learned all that in Hebrew school."

"So you know about organizations like the Haganah, Irgun, and how they eventually turned into what we know today as the IDF, Mossad, and Shin Bet?"

"Kind of."

"What most people don't know is that when the defenses of the Jewish state evolved, there was a parallel organized effort to protect Jewish people in places where they were being threatened. Initially it was all focused on facilitating immigration to Palestine, also known as the 'Aliyah,' but the focus broadened when people found that not everybody was ready to pack up and leave. Many of the organizations cooperating in this are informal, sometimes transient, and are being set up as needed. At one point, people were hoping to have a common organization under the roof of the Jewish Defense League, but when that organization turned radical, they simply continued as before—with just informal ties to the organizations in Israel that were willing to lend a hand.

"I am part of such a group that is loosely linked to the Mossad. Most of the time, we protect. Sometimes we help gather information. Sometimes we recruit. You came on our radar because of some work your father did in the past; he might want to fill you in on that in more detail. As far as I'm concerned, I was supposed to try and establish contact with him, and you were the only lead we had at the time. So I transferred to Syracuse on a falsified student record as Sara Baur.

"We found your father through a different connection, and I was able to contact him when he was just about to look into some old unfinished business. What he found seems to have the potential to rattle a lot of cages that are occupied by some pretty unpleasant animals. In addition, he was recalled to his old job under what he thinks is a pretense. He suspects that it has to do with the same topic. He wants you out of reach of people who have an interest in using you to blackmail him."

"Who wants to blackmail him?"

"I don't think he knows yet. At this point, he just wants to make sure it can't happen."

"So my father is working for your organization as well?" They never talked openly about the exact nature of her father's job, but Nicole had always been pretty sure that he was part of some US government agency.

"He does not. I'm not sure if I am supposed to tell you this, but your father works for the CIA and has been in semiretirement for the last five years. After the attack on your family, the agency decided to send you into a falsified witness protection program, and your father was kept in a mountain cabin in Spain."

"Why?"

"I can only speculate."

"It's a long drive—lots of time to speculate."

"Okay then. The obvious reason is that he needed to be kept both safe and accessible. Sending him into witness protection with you would have made it close to impossible for the agency to use his skills. But as he tells the story, they have not used their access and instead left him in a retired state. So my suspicion is they had unresolved issues they were trying to clear up while he was out of the way. Once this is done, they will likely come up with a decision what to do about him. But as I said, it's all speculation. I don't think he knows either."

Nicole decided this was as good a time as any to bring up a topic that had bothered her for a long time. "So if your assignment was to watch me and find my father, what in the hell were you thinking when you stole my boyfriend?"

"In part it was to protect you. Jeff is a total jerk."

"So you figured you'd sacrifice yourself instead? How generous."

"The other reason was we had to get him out of the way. It made room for Josh to connect with you."

"Josh was your boyfriend at the time."

"He actually never was. We just staged all that to make it easier for him to connect with you."

"So for Josh, I was a job?"

"Initially yes. Something must have changed about half a year ago. We were about to reassign him after we found that he had gotten too deeply involved. But then I had to leave and our only choice was to leave Josh to watch you for the last few weeks."

Nicole thought back to what might have happened six months earlier but couldn't really think of anything that would explain what Nora just said.

"One more thing about Josh: he will defend you with all he has. I should probably not tell you this, but if you end up needing serious help, he's the one to turn to."

"One more question: What happened to my phone?"

"I gave it to one of the street kids in Paris. They will use it until the SIM card runs dry and then sell it to someone else."

"Are you insane? That was a brand-new iPhone!"

"Yup, which makes it more likely that it will travel for a while. That's precisely what we need."

"Why?"

"Because it will be tracked, and we'd rather throw them off your track for a while."

"It can't be tracked. I left my SIM card at home and put a new one in when I arrived in Paris."

"You are watching too much TV. The SIM card holds your caller ID, and it links the phone to your account with your cell phone company. If you really want to track a phone, you use the device ID instead. It does not change just because you use it under a new account. Your path this morning will be tracked to the restaurant where we met. Then they will follow the phone to some place in Paris and will scare the bejeezus out of some kid in the suburbs who just bought a cheap phone. After that they know you intentionally ditched them and the hunt is on. But this buys us about three to four days."

"And who is the 'they' in this?"

"If we are lucky, we will never know."

"And if not?"

"Let's just hope you'll never find out."

"So you don't know."

"Not yet. But there are only a few candidates. None of them is a pleasant option."

Nicole realized what was different about Nora since she last saw her. "What happened to your face?"

"I had a bit of a falling out with someone I tried to get information from."

"I hope it didn't have anything to do with my father?"

"No. Actually he helped me out of a jam on that occasion."

"Are those the kinds of people to expect?"

"Nope. That was what we'd consider a reasonably friendly encounter."

Nicole thought about what she heard so far. She didn't like a single bit of it. But she was a realist enough to know that there was little she could do about it. Instead, she decided to change the topic.

"So how is working with my father?"

"I guess not so bad, if you like to be kept in the dark, told what to do, and enjoy monosyllabic grunts instead of lavish praise when you do something to his satisfaction."

For the first time today Nicole felt a sense of comic relief. "I guess I can confirm that you found the real David Monthausser."

Chapter 8

David arrived at his sister's ski apartment just after lunch. Yasemin opened the door, clearly not thrilled to see him.

"Can I speak to Erdal?"

"He's not here."

"Where can I find him? It's urgent."

Yasemin's expression switched from annoyed to worried. "When you say urgent, it always means trouble."

"I hope not, but I have to talk to him quickly."

"He should be back tomorrow. You can stay until then, if you want—it's your house, sort of."

"Any idea where he went?"

"He said he would not be far. He can't be since he does not have a car."

David thought for a minute. He knew the only public transport in Valberg was the bus line that connected the town to Nice. Erdal could have hitchhiked, which was not that unusual here in the mountains, but David didn't think he would. To Yasemin, he said, "I'll be back tomorrow."

David drove to the bus terminal next to the base station for the ski lift and checked the schedule and itinerary for the TER buses. There was only one line, and it went through the Gorges du Cians, a deep canyon lined with red limestone, to the town of Touët in the Var valley and would then follow the valley south to the Nice airport. The only towns along the bus line were tiny farming communities—not a single one that David thought of as a potential destination for Erdal. He figured Erdal was meeting someone in downtown Nice, in which case he'd have to take the bus to the airport and connect from there. Finding him in Nice would be hopeless, but if he wanted to be back tomorrow, there was only a single bus he could take from the airport. David decided to try his luck there.

When he checked into the airport hotel, he noticed a crowd of people standing at the TV monitors. Some were American tourists who had just flown in and some were local businessmen. Apparently, an SUV loaded with explosives had been dis-covered in an underground parking lot at the Mall of America in Bloomington, Minnesota. The news reported that the bomb was linked to a sleeper cell of four young Pakistani men who had lived in Minnesota for almost their entire lives, were devout Muslims, had no criminal record, and according to their neigh-bors were "always friendly, nice young men."

One of the locals commented liberally on the news, explain-ing to whoever wanted to hear it that he was not surprised about this mess, that the Pakistanis were the American version of "les Arabes" around here, and that they were all just taking advantage of the liberal western societies while they were wait-ing to see how they could bite the hands that kept feeding them. David noticed a Front National sticker on his jacket and cringed. One of the American tourists spoke enough French to get into a discussion with the FN activist and explained that he lived in a town with a large Muslim population and none of them was ever giving them any trouble. David knew how this would end, and predictably the FN man answered, "See, and you make it easy for them closing your eyes even when the problem is totally obvious."

David felt sick. But he hoped the e-mail he had sent a few days earlier would now be remembered by someone who cared.

SAINT PAUL, MINNESOTA.

Judith Ingersson heard the news about the arrest and the bombing plot from her TV over breakfast. Her two kids were fighting over something they heard in school and she had to use what her older son usually described as her "cranky voice" to shut them up so she could hear the details. As the news was continuing, she realized she knew all the details before the an-nouncer said the words. The e-mail she decided to save as a well-written and particularly funny specimen of completely out-rageous conspiracy theory was the real thing. She opened her laptop, found the message, and typed a six-word response: "Where and when can we meet?" She had a response within five seconds: "Mail server delivery problem: E-mail account not valid."

Later in the day, she spoke to her paper's IT support person who had helped her with tricky and sometimes barely legal networking problems in the past. He asked to see the e-mail, changed the settings to see the full header, and quickly gave his assessment: "You're not getting anything from this."

"Why not?"

"Whoever this is really does not want to be found. They are using a service called 'Tor' that hides the trail the data packets traveled on. It is not possible to locate where the e-mail came from, even if we were to go back to the log files on the e-mail server and analyzed each data packet. And I'm guessing they also deleted the e-mail account right after they sent the mail to you."

"But we could check with their e-mail provider who owned the account, right?"

"If we felt like hacking Gmail, yes. But since Gmail does not verify the account holder's information, they might as well call themselves Dick Cheney—Google won't care." He knew her dislike of the former vice president all too well—she routinely called him "Vice" in her columns.

"So then how about this anonymizer service—'Tor' was it?"

"Same thing there. Not that we could hack them to begin with, but if we could, I bet we'd find that they accessed it with a spoofed IP address as a second layer of protection. Plus, knowing how they signed in would do us no good since Tor wipes all traces of the activity that runs through it."

"So I'm stuck."

"It depends. Clearly this was meant as a one-way e-mail. So the question is what did they want?"

"Well, they couldn't expect me to publish based on this information. Clearly they are smarter than that."

"Right. So my guess is, it was meant as an introduction. Sort of to establish their credentials. In other words, you should expect more."

"But I need to establish a two-way communication. Without being able to ask questions, I don't think I can trust this source. It would be opening myself for manipulation."

"There is one thing you can try. I assume they create an account only to send the mail and then they close it immediately. So by the time you read the mail, they are already logged off and gone. But what if we can figure out some pattern that identifies the incoming mail and then write an e-mail rule that fires off an immediate auto-response?"

"Like an out-of-office reply?"

"Sort of. But it would only get triggered when you receive a message from someone who uses an anonymizer service and when it has certain keywords in it."

"You're thinking they might reuse some of the wording to make sure I recognize them."

"Exactly. This one started with something like 'Do Not Delete,' right?"

"Yes."

"So let me work on the mail rule for a little bit, and I'll set something up that shoots off an instant response—all you have to do is fill it with the content you want them to see. How's that?"

"Perfect."

In the meantime Judith decided to call her ex-husband at the Bloomington Police Department. She knew he was now one of the senior detectives on the squad, and she figured he'd likely be involved in the bombing case.

"Hey, John, do you have a second to talk?"

"Not really. I know you want to ask me about the bombing, and you need to come to the press conference at noon like everybody else."

"I'm not calling to ask. I have something I want to run by you."

"Make it quick."

"I know you are not releasing things like the license plate of the car involved. But can I read it to you?"

"I don't understand."

She read the license plate number from the e-mail she received and got the expected reaction: John burst out, "How the hell..." before he caught himself and added, "I can't comment on this and you know it."

"I don't need a comment. I was just looking for confirmation. Thanks, I owe you."

LANGLEY. HENRY FLETCHER'S OFFICE.

"Henry, we have a serious problem."

Henry never liked Dick Mulligan, the director of asset protection. What a stupid title to begin with. Plus, he thought Dick was a pompous ass. Between his obsessive need to show up in a bow tie and tweed jacket all the time and his way of talking as if nothing mattered outside his narrow jurisdiction, Henry was fed up with him the moment he walked through the door. Out loud he said, "Well, then how can I help make it less serious?"

"Remember the girl we placed in witness protection five years ago?"

"Five years ago? Come on, Dick."

"Her name is Erica van Wyden." He had Henry's attention now.

"What about her?"

"She skipped town."

"Meaning what?"

"She drove to Canada to attend a concert."

"Oh, come on—big deal."

"And then boarded a flight to Paris." *Paris, damn.*

"You had a babysitter working on the case, didn't you?"

"Yes." Dick clearly had more information but kept quiet.

"So what did he see?"

"He only found out about it today."

Henry stared at him waiting for further explanations.

Dick started to squirm. "He followed her to some party that went until four in the morning, overheard her talking about sleeping in the next day, so he decided to do the same. He was looking for her on campus but didn't see her. Then today, he called me saying she was gone."

Henry raised an eyebrow and wanted to know, "And how does he know?"

"Apparently, Ms. van Wyden posted a message on her Facebook page that she ran into friends from Switzerland and is joining them for a few days in the mountains." *All the surveillance we pay for, and then we find out via fucking Facebook*. Henry was royally pissed.

"Well?"

"We have no record of such friends."

"She flew to Paris, you said?"

"Yes. And we have monitored her cell phone. She switched SIM cards for a prepaid card. But we are tracking the phone."

"Prepaid cards avoid roaming charges. My kids do that all the time when they go to Europe."

Mulligan seemed off track; apparently he never spent much time abroad. "Anyway, the phone is not in Switzerland."

"Is it in Paris?"

"No. It is in a small town in the Alsace."

"Not far from Switzerland."

"Is it?"

Jeeze, Dick. You already know about Facebook, how about Google Maps! "Yes. I assume you checked whether there is a record of Ms. van Wyden crossing the border?"

"We tried asking the Swiss nicely and they refused to tell us."

Henry thought of all the recent trouble the United States had caused the Swiss about the banking laws and didn't really have to guess why they'd be so obstinate. "Then I suspect you asked less nicely?"

"We didn't bother asking a second time. We just checked their records directly. There is nothing." Now Dick looked at Henry triumphantly, as if he wanted to say *quot errat demonstrandum*.

"As I remember it, we issued Ms. van Wyden a Dutch passport and made her a foreign student, right?"

"Yes."

"So her passport was issued by the European Union, and if she traveled to Switzerland by car, the border guards would in ninety-nine percent of all cases simply wave her through when they see the cover of the passport. Or if she traveled by train, she would never see a border guard to begin with."

"Except she'd still have to register somewhere to stay overnight."

"Not if she's really visiting friends."

Dick looked positively irritated. Then he tried his last attempt: "But the phone..."

"How do you know she didn't lose it on the train to Basel or something?"

"Where is Basel?"

"So I assume you will find her, and when she comes back, you will give her a lecture about checking in with her witness protection officer before leaving?"

Mulligan was embarrassed and left fuming. But Henry was not satisfied. Had this happened any other time, he would have already forgotten about the incident. But with David being reactivated and his boss pushing hard to find David's old contact and the other members of his terror cell, he thought he couldn't just ignore it. He called James to ask for the full record of Erica van Wyden's phone trace.

Looking at the trace document, he did not see a lot that would raise suspicions. The phone was mostly inactive when she landed in Paris except for a search in Google Maps. As expected, the phone then traveled to the destination searched for. It stayed there for almost an hour, then traveled across Paris, zigzagged a few more times, made a fair amount of phone calls to local numbers, then traveled at high speed to Mulhouse, and then to a small town called Guebwiller. Henry figured, given the travel speed, the phone and possibly its owner were on a TGV train.

So what was the story here? She must have met someone at a restaurant in the center of Paris. After that, she made five phone calls, all local numbers and all registered in the phone book under various French names. Boyfriends? Not likely. Leaving messages for people? Maybe. But then she gets on a train to Mulhouse. Something was not right.

He figured Nicole would be in contact with her father. If so, her real purpose was to meet him in Europe. If he was right, she would have to contact him. What if one of these local numbers was a dead-letter voice mail? He called all five of them. Each time, some French person picked up but did not know any Erica or Nicole. He decided to dig deeper and picked up the phone.

"Hey, Frank, how is everything going in your shop?"

"You really don't want to know—what a mess."

"Still cleaning up after Mr. Snowden?"

"Worse than that. But I suspect that's not what you are calling about. What do you need?"

"See, that's the problem. I don't exactly know. I have a cell phone number that was traveling in Paris, and I need to find other phones in its proximity to see if there is a connection."

"Henry, you know you need to send me a formal request. They've tightened the rules around this kind of snooping for a good reason."

"Shit, man, if I knew what to put in a formal query, I'd be much better off already. I need to look at things to see if an inspiration comes up. Look, I'm not interested in the content of any phone calls, all I need is the metadata."

"I can't just give you access; they'll slap my wrist again."

"What if I come over and take a look at your place?"

"I suppose…"

Henry didn't like the idea of driving to Fort Meade, but he did not think he had a choice.

When he got to Frank's office, Frank was just about to run out.

"I'm about to go get some lunch—should I bring anything back for you?"

"No, thanks—I'm a bit in a hurry. Can I…"

"I will be back in half an hour. Don't touch anything, okay?"

Henry followed Frank's nod toward his computer, which had the search screen for the phone database open. "Understood." In other word, if anybody were to check later, Frank would have his cafeteria receipt to proof that he was not in his office when the offending search was made. *Plausible deniability it is, then*.

Once Frank had left, Henry went to work. He already had the path Nicole's phone had taken through Paris and the time stamps for each location. His suspicion was that she must have met someone, possibly David, at one of her stops. Whoever it was would have an untraceable phone with them. So his first step was to find phones that were in close proximity and had a prepaid card. He eliminated the ones that seemed to be simply traveling on the same metro line. His result showed three clusters of phones with prepaid cards—one in or close to an apartment in the northern suburbs; one near the Place de la Concorde; and a third one near a restaurant called l'Ilot Vache.

His next step restricted the result further by checking which of the prepaid phones made phone calls during the time they were meeting up with Nicole's phone. He ended up with a list of only five phones, three of them at the restaurant. He knew it was a long shot, but he checked the target numbers and found one that had called another burner phone. *Got you!* He guessed that David did not want to handle the pickup himself but had sent someone who called him to confirm. So David's phone had to be the target and whoever met Nicole probably brought further instructions. He needed to have a discussion with some people.

Frank came back with a sandwich in hand. "What did I miss?"

"Somebody asking about phone numbers in Paris." Henry used his mischievous grin to signal "nothing to worry about."

"Anything I need to know in case someone asks?"

"Unlikely. But I asked you about someone we had placed in witness protection who was traveling to Paris, right?"

"I believe you did. Did I check who was in contact with her phone?"

"That and who was in the neighborhood."

"I'm not getting any questions from our watchdogs, am I?"

"Unlikely. It's all anonymous phones. You didn't violate anybody's privacy."

"Always good to know."

LANGLEY, CONFERENCE ROOM.

"Henry, you know we have to bring him in—including his daughter. It's far too risky to let them run wild out there."

Henry had never liked Ron. Ron's career had been fast-tracked when he found himself on the same side as the so-called neoconservatives who wanted nothing more than finding a reason to go to war against Iraq and were perfectly willing to manufacture evidence to give politicians some extra incentive. His boss, Victoria Feltner, had brought Ron into the discussion against his objection pointing out that it was better to brief him now than having him scream bloody murder if he found out later.

Besides having an unseemly disrespect for other human beings, Ron Polanyi, or Ron the Hun as David used to call him, also suffered from an insatiable appetite for power and would best be kept on a remote island without any connection to the rest of the world, if Henry had his way. "We can't disrupt what David is doing now just because we have a hunch—there is no hard data for anything."

"Have you called and confronted him?"

"There is no good outcome from a confrontation strategy. If he is up to something, we tip him off. And if not, we alienate him for no good reason."

"I'll say it's good reason, all right." Ron's dislike of David was well known everywhere in the agency. The two had a very public blowup over David's Anderssen Gambit paper when Ron advocated using the strategies outlined in the paper offensively. David had argued that this would be highly irresponsible and would amount to an egregious abuse of power by the agency—a notion that sounded utterly ridiculous to Ron.

Victoria settled the issue. "Henry will meet with David in Europe. Location is up to you. You know him best—look him in the eyes when you ask him whether he knows where his daughter is and determine what to do after that. I trust your judgment on this one."

Ron tried one more time and suggested that he should be there as well. But Victoria wanted to hear none of it.

NEXT MORNING. NICE, AIRPORT BUS TERMINAL.

David sat across from the bus terminal for the regional bus lines and immersed himself in the morning's edition of the local paper called *Nice Matin*. He spotted Erdal walking from one of the buses coming in from city center and walked behind him on the way to the TER bus.

"Bonjour, Monsieur Brahimi."

Erdal was clearly on edge, but he calmed down when he realized it was David. However, he did not say anything.

"I can give you a ride. I am parked across the street."

Erdal did not argue and followed him to the car.

"So how is everything going with Hani?" David's casual tone could not mask the fact that he knew he was stepping on a potential land mine.

Erdal looked at him from the passenger seat and took a while before answering. "Depends on how you look at it."

David detected an undercurrent of hostility in Erdal's voice and decided to tread lightly. "Look, I expected you to get in touch with him, and I'm glad you did. I'm just trying to get a read on what his thoughts are on this mess."

"It's a mess all right. From what I'm hearing, you are supposed to bring me in, right?"

"I am indeed, but I haven't done it yet, have I?"

"Hani thinks he has pretty solid information that you are deeply involved in the plot to subvert the secret services of most industrialized nations. It is a power grab involving blackmail of lawmakers all over the western world. Much more effective than a coup d'état, since they have no need to run the countries directly—it's far more convenient to do so by controlling politicians who act as their cardboard cutouts."

David thought about what he had read in Bromberger's files and couldn't really disagree with Hani's assessment. But he was surprised by Erdal's conclusion. "Why do you think I'm involved?"

"For starters, you wrote the paper on it. But he also says you're associated with the hardline faction that wants to establish what they call a dictatorship of the agencies—sort of like a Dick Cheney on steroids."

"He is right that I wrote the original paper that was used as guide. But I have nothing to do with what is currently being run. I was sidelined for the last five years. What does Hani's side of things look like?"

"He says he is being pressured by his KGB pals, or FSB as they call themselves now, to turn in to headquarters."

"Tell him not to."

"I did. David, what the hell are you up to? I thought we were always pulling in the same direction, making the world a place where normal people can just go about their lives without tyranny or fear of governments run amok."

"I never lied to you. And I think the reason why I'm reactivated has to do with someone trying to finally stick their head out against these people. I still don't know who is who, but I will find out."

One of David's burner phones rang. He asked Erdal to pull it out of his bag and put it on speaker while he was driving.

"David? Where are you?"

Hearing Henry's voice on the phone that only Nora was supposed to know about was not welcome news. "Driving north outside of Nice. Why?" *How the hell did he get this number?*

"I need to meet with you. Mulhouse airport tomorrow morning. I will come in on a flight around eight."

"Mulhouse is a six-hour drive from here. What is going on?"

"We will talk then."

Henry had hung up. Erdal looked at David. "You're pale as a ghost."

"He was not supposed to have this number."

"How often have you used it?"

"Once."

"Wow. Who did you call on it? And what's going on in Mulhouse?"

"Not a clue. It could be a setup. Or he might need help. I'm not sure which."

"Only one way to find out."

"Look, I know you have your doubts about my motivation. Can you drive with me to Mulhouse and back me up? It's a long drive. I can fill you in on everything I know at this point."

Erdal said nothing for a long time. Then, "I need to talk with Yasemin first. And I need to make one call to Hani."

"Can I talk to him?"

"Not a good idea. One more question. Who was this one the phone?"

"Henry Fletcher, my boss at the CIA. Why?"

"Because I have heard his voice before."

"Where?"

"On Hani's conference call yesterday."

David felt sweat building on his forehead. "What did he have to say?"

"Nothing until the end. And then only one question. He wanted to know how to find me. Hani told him his last contact with me was five years ago."

"Who else was on the call?"

"Just Hani's FSB boys."

Bad news. Clearly Henry was in contact with the FSB and knew about the real constellation of the alleged terror group. It also meant he was spoon-feeding a bunch of horse manure to David to get him to find Erdal—something that apparently could not be done via the FSB connection. "Why is the FSB protecting you from us?"

"They are not. Hani has given them the same answer. He says the FSB has asked him to bring me to Moscow as soon as he can find me."

"You're a popular man these days. Everybody wants a piece of you. What do you have that they think is so valuable?"

"I wish I knew. I was hoping Hani could shed some light on it, but he seemed to have no idea either."

After filling in Erdal on most of what he knew at this point, David figured he needed one more piece of crucial information to prepare for his meeting with Henry. But it was too early to get it. He had to wait until late at night when Henry's plane to Europe would have taken off.

At 3:00 a.m., he called Angela from his official CIA phone.

"Hi, Angela."

"David—what a pleasant surprise."

"Henry called me earlier. I was driving at the time and then the call got dropped. If I heard correctly, he wanted me to meet him in Mulhouse, but the details were garbled. And now I can't reach him—I suspect his flight has already taken off."

"I didn't know Henry was traveling." She was wondering why David called her about this rather than Henry's assistant Jenna. Then she realized: he wanted her to find out what was really going on.

"I'm pretty sure he is since I'm supposed to meet him. Could you check the details?" He hoped she would understand 'details' as a request for information about the size of the travel party and any information about the purpose.

"I'm in the middle of something. But can I call you back in an hour?"

Good, she understood. "Certainly."

An hour later, Angela was on the phone again, and this time she sounded worried.

"I couldn't find Henry's travel plan in the official record. No commercial ticket and no flight plan filed for any of the agency jets."

"Okay, so how is he getting here?"

"Do you know a company called Shenandoah Information Security?"

"No."

"They are one of our temporary shells. They own a Gulfstream V, and he has it checked out under the name of one of the company executives."

The CIA used shell companies for many purposes: to move money, to run a fleet of private airplanes without them being associated with the US government, and to provide a facade for cyberattacks among other things. A few months later Shenandoah Information Services would be dismantled or declared bankrupt and its assets bought out by some other freshly created shell company. If anybody ever tried to follow the trail of any specific asset, whether it was an airplane or an IP address or a temporary employee, they would ultimately find nothing but empty shells of companies that did not exist anymore, and none of their owners or employees could be reached.

Henry asked, "Anybody else coming?"

"Not on the same flight. But a second Gulfstream is en route as well with Ron on board, plus an additional four passengers. They are two hours behind."

This could only mean one thing: Henry thought he was meeting with him in private, but Ron the Hun was about to crash the party with a SWAT team in tow. "I assume you are being careful?"

"David, you taught me well." She had accessed Henry's computer remotely using Henry's ssh key. She had swiped it previously when Henry had asked her for help with some networking problem. She also knew any remote login would be tracked and recorded, but she wiped her trail after she was done—or at least she thought she had wiped it.

"Let's hope so."

Chapter 9

WEDNESDAY MORNING, MULHOUSE AIRPORT.

Henry had asked to meet at a bar called "Trib's" in the arrival hall in the French section of Mulhouse airport. But in the light of what he had found out, David had no intention of letting Henry pick the meeting location. He had called a car service to pick Henry up when he came through customs. The sign would read "Boris Ivanovich Fedorov"—one of Henry's long retired aliases he used during the times of the Cold War. Just to make sure, he also texted Henry's picture to the driver and asked him to look for him, explaining that Boris Ivanovich might not be looking for a pickup.

He was still wondering what to do about the second airplane when Erdal said, "Do you need to be worried about more than one person arriving?"

"Actually, yes. Why?"

"I have a friend who works in air traffic control. I might be able to get some details."

"You mean from the flight manifest?"

"Yes."

"I know it's just Henry and the pilot. But there is a second flight with a total of five passengers. That's what I'm more worried about. Do you think your friend can find out its schedule?"

"Do you know the airplane's tags?"

"Unfortunately no, but it's a Gulfstream owned by a company called Shenandoah Information Services, and it should be about two hours behind the first one."

"That should be good enough to find it."

Erdal would stay in contact with his friend until the second airplane was about to land, then text David a warning and meet him at the Café zum Roten Engel in downtown Basel.

Henry passed the customs gate at 6:30 a.m., planning to walk straight to Trib's in the arrival hall. As he was walking through the nearly empty hall, he was stopped by a limousine driver holding a sign. "Excusez moi, Monsieur Fedorov?"

Henry gave him a blank stare, then recognized the name as one of his old aliases, but said, "I am not looking for a car, thank you."

"Your colleague has asked me to drive you to your meeting."

When Henry and the driver got to the car, David was waiting in the backseat. He put his finger across his lips, signaling to Henry to stay quiet. The driver asked, "A Mulhouse?" David answered, "Oui." They took the main highway toward town, but at the second exit, David asked the driver to take the exit for a town called Kembs and had him drop them off halfway between the highway and the town at a muddy forestry road. David held out his hand with his phone in it, gesturing to Henry to do the same. After he collected all phones and other electronics and left them in the front passenger seat, he told the driver to continue to the Mulhouse Zoo. He handed him a written note that read, "Be back here in ninety minutes, turn the radio on loud, please." The driver just shrugged—he thought he had seen it all during his career, but this one certainly was a bit strange.

LANGLEY, MONITORING ROOM.

"James, how is Henry's meeting with David going?"

"It looks like they met, but not quite as expected." James didn't particularly like the young kid from Ron the Hun's department. But he had to admit that it was guilt by association—what he really couldn't stand was Ron and his habit of absorbing everybody's energy and time. There was little that James valued more than being able to keep things predictable. Whenever he had business with Ron, it meant something had gone horribly wrong, and it threw off everybody's schedule.

"Not quite as expected—what does that mean?"

"Not in the café—instead they are driving to the city."

"Turn on the audio."

"It's on."

"Why can't we hear anything?"

"Because nobody is talking."

"Why?"

"You want me to ask them? Hold on, listen."

They heard David tell the driver to continue to Mulhouse. After that the radio was turned on and all they heard was a local radio station blasting French music with the occasional static and possibly voices in the background, but it might have been just the static from the FM station.

"What's going on?"

James raised an eyebrow—he hated it when he had to explain what he thought was totally obvious. "Someone turned on the radio."

When they started walking in the forest, David picked up a ziplock bag under a bush and took out the phone that he put there earlier in the morning. He checked for messages from Erdal and found one that read, "2nd plane over Shannon, IE." He knew he had about sixty minutes before Ron's crew arrived and ninety minutes before they'd exit the airport.

"Okay, why are you here?"

"Because I need to find out what's going on. We know Nicole left the US and is hiding in Guebwiller. We think you have sent her there."

David was relieved—clearly Nora's cell phone diversion showed some interesting results. To Henry he said, "Where in the world is Guebwiller?"

"Twenty minutes north of here."

David had to laugh. "Is this why you wanted me to show up in Mulhouse?"

"Yes, and to get an opportunity to talk to you in person."

"Okay, now that I'm here, talk."

"Look, this doesn't have to be such a standoff. I'm trying to find out what's going on. Besides, we do know that Nicole is in Europe."

"Henry, you are the one who parked her in your stupid witness protection program. If you're telling me you lost her, you had better go find her or I'll make your life miserable. If you think she's in Guebwiller, why don't you take the car when it comes back and go visit her? Better yet, I'll come with you—I haven't seen her in years, after all."

"I may do that. In the meantime, how is your investigation going?"

"Jeeze, Henry, I am on my second day looking into a five-year-old cold case. How much do you expect me to find so quickly?"

"I can hope, can't I?"

"I found a few hints, but nothing that I would consider established facts."

"Wanna let me in on them?"

David hadn't planned on it, but he figured he might as well shoot off a trial balloon. "All I know so far is that the group that we thought was a terror cell wasn't quite what it seemed."

"How do you mean?"

"According to some sources who looked into the matter at the time, we weren't the only ones who infiltrated the group. One source went so far to say it looked more like a conference of secret services than an al-Qaeda group."

"You spoke to your contact in MIT?" The Milli Istihbarat Teskilati was the Turkish national intelligence service where David had a contact in the past. Henry never knew the identity of his contact and was likely unaware that Bülent had died two years ago. David decided to keep the source mysterious.

"MIT and some others. Everybody is wondering why we are interested. They seem to agree that the cell was set up as a front. Not that this makes a lot of sense to me."

"I think it does to me. I don't have hard data either, but from what I heard, the Russians had started it as a front to co-operate with the Iranians, the Syrians, and possibly others. It followed the same script you had outlined in your controversial document. When you infiltrated the group with Erdal's help, we didn't know. But we think it is still used like this, either with or without Erdal, but we need him to fill us in."

"Funny, one of the people I spoke to said the FSB is looking for him as well."

"I'm not surprised. They probably figured out who he really is."

What kind of game are you playing? David wasn't sure where Henry stood, so he looked straight at him and asked, "Are you in contact with the FSB?"

"On this topic?"

David saw Henry's nervous reaction and decided he had heard enough. Henry's acting skills had never been very good. "Why wasn't I given the real story?"

"After you wrote your document, it was circulated among the neocon crowd inside the agency as their game plan evolved to dominate the agency and then far more than just the agency. They were trying to turn it into a blueprint for how to turn a country into a secret service dictatorship while leaving all the institutions in place and making it appear as if they'd still be functioning as before. They saw their chance to control the country without having to resort to any of the nasty means that dictators of the past had to use. It was essentially Stalin without the need for gulags.

"After you had your public blowout with them, it appeared at first as if the executive floor had come to their senses and reined them in. But then small things changed. We all noticed that at regular intervals terror plots would be uncovered. They were all found just before something was expected to explode and we thought, 'How come we are so lucky?'

"It appeared to keep working miraculously. A short time after that my job in the science and technology group started to change. Instead of defending against intruders, we started creating our own intrusions and uncovering them at the same time. We are actually pretty good at it, too. In the past SigInt was mostly concentrating on figuring out what our enemies were talking about when they thought we weren't listening. Today, we don't care who the bad guys are. We just record everything and once we know what we are looking for, we search for keywords and filter down from a massive search result via exclusion criteria. The problem is we never find enough, so we always have to make up some stuff to keep the threat potential high. Otherwise, Congress will cut funding.

"The best part of it is, this works across borders and without having to explicitly mention it. Everybody seems to naturally understand how it works. The only ones who are a bit obstinate about it are the Germans and the French."

"So you are trying to tell me that you are willing to disable all the institutions in the democracy that we've been sworn to protect?" David still remembered Henry's outrage when Ron the Hun and his cronies manufactured evidence that eventually led to the Iraq war. His point at the time was that the job of the agency was to find solid facts so that politicians could build an opinion and then make a decision where to take the country. He had all but accused Ron of being a fascist dictator.

"No. I'm giving you an assessment of what has happened in the agency since you left. I'm also admitting that I'm powerless to stop it."

David looked at Henry and noticed he looked truly embarrassed. But one thing was still bothering him: "Then why are you dealing with the Russians in this?"

"Because I need to find Erdal, and I'm willing to find help wherever I can get it."

"Even from Ron the Hun."

"What do you mean?"

David checked the text that had just come in. "He just landed in Mulhouse."

Henry looked truly worried. "Then we need to move."

"No. I need to move. All you have to do is go back, run into him at the airport after having finished your meeting, and act surprised."

"He will come after you—and after Nicole."

"I'll worry about myself, if you don't mind. Oh, and one more question: If the terror cell was a Russian front, how come Erdal was able to infiltrate it masked as an Islamic extremist?"

"You should ask him when you find him."

David knew that Hani had recruited him and he had his suspicion about what that meant, but he wanted to know whether Henry knew.

They found the car where it had dropped them off. While Henry got into the backseat, David took their CIA phones, figuring that Ron would be tracking them. He stopped a farmer's tractor that was passing them and asked the old man for directions to Strassbourg. He was told to get back to the highway, drive toward Mulhouse, and then keep straight north. David thanked the farmer and shook his right hand while his left hand poked the phones into his load of freshly harvested hay.

LANGLEY, MONITORING ROOM.

"James, audio is back."

"In French, though."

"Someone is asking for directions to Strassbourg."

"Quiet again."

"Yes, but check where the signal is going."

"Toward the river—if they follow it north, it goes indeed straight to Strassbourg."

"Yes, but at this speed it will take them three days before they get there."

"Does this make any sense to you?"

"Nope. Just patch the location through to Ron as he asked."

After saying good-bye to Henry and making sure he actually went through security to his airplane, David passed through customs to the Swiss side of the airport and called a cab to meet Erdal in downtown Basel.

Ron and his team were getting ready in a car that had been sent fully equipped by the CIA station chief in Paris.

"Are you getting a signal from our friends?"

"Loud and clear."

"How far away?"

"Not far at all. Both phones are close to each other, moving slowly in an unpopulated area. Looks like they are probably walking through a forest or through fields. James says the last audio they picked up from the phones seems to indicate they are moving toward Strassbourg, but their speed is close to walking speed."

They followed the country roads toward the village of Kembs, where the signal led them through fields and pastures.

Ron inquired: "What's going on?"

Their van had stopped at a small farm; the signal pointed toward a shed.

"Are they in there?"

"Yup."

"Any way we can get eyes on them?"

"Probably better if we just bust in."

Across the yard, Michelle Voeckler saw a van pull up next to her husband's machine shed and panicked when five bullnecked men got out of the car and took weapons out of the trunk. She dialed 112, the police emergency number.

The shed had a large door to allow tractors and other machinery to get through and a smaller one on the side. They decided to kick down the small door and leave two men outside in case someone wanted to make a run for it.

Ron heard the sirens first. "It's now or never."

They had just kicked in the small door when the first police car pulled into the farm's inner yard, a second one following.

After a short but very tense standoff with weapons drawn on both sides, more police cars pulled up and it became rather obvious their only way out was by spending some quality time in the custody of the French Gendarmerie.

Ron was extremely upset. "How the fuck could this happen?"

The leader of the swat team knew: "Only one way: they knew we were coming."

FRIDAY AFTERNOON, LANGLEY. VICTORIA FELTNER'S OFFICE.

People who didn't know Victoria always misinterpreted her calmness as not being rattled easily. Henry knew better: right now she was furious.

"So can either one of you clue me in on how you coordinated your visits to Mulhouse yesterday?"

Ron decided it was better to take the bull by the horns. "We didn't since we figured it was better if we picked up David without giving him any warning."

"And how did that work for you?"

"He evaded capture, which I think is clear evidence that he turned against us and needs to be treated as hostile."

"Clear evidence? Really? The only clear evidence I have is that five of my agents were arrested by French police, called the consulate for diplomatic support, and managed to get one agent released since he was traveling on a fake diplomatic passport. The other four are still in custody and the French are asking whether we are planning to invade their country, given the arsenal of weapons they found in the trunk of your fucking car. Ten minutes ago, the French ambassador sent a very sour diplomatic note to our secretary of state, in which he indicates that he knows the passport used by the released agent was fake and is asking for his immediate arrest and extradition on espionage charges."

"The US government doesn't extradite its citizens when they are accused of spying by a foreign nation."

"Indeed. But it does get royally embarrassed when it has to choose between admitting that its secretive agencies have committed crimes and pretending that it knows nothing. There is no good course of action here."

Even Ron knew that there was no excuse in this case. He had fucked up. Royally. Henry knew what this meant. Ron would take it out on whoever got in his way next, and he was the primary target. He tried to steer the conversation in a different direction. "I think we should simply let this run, give David a chance to connect with some of his past contacts, and see what he comes up with."

Ron shot him a look that indicated "you liberal son-of-a-bitch, where I come from we interrogate people, we don't let them run around Europe." Aloud he said, "Only if we want him to create more damage."

Victoria was getting exasperated. "Damage? What did he do so far?"

Ron jumped right in: "He evacuated his daughter from our jurisdiction and is clearly preparing to defect. We need to get him and find out what he is up to as soon as possible."

Henry was alarmed: "There is absolutely no evidence that he is even in contact with his daughter."

"Then why don't you bring her back and make sure of that?"

"With all due respect, I do not consider that a priority. She is visiting friends and the only thing she did wrong was not tell her witness protection officer—who from what I'm hearing has not even checked in with her in over twelve months, so it's hardly surprising that she would forget."

"She is evading your monitoring attempts, isn't she?"

"Her phone was very likely stolen. Nothing else."

"But you don't know this, do you?"

Henry had to admit, "Not for sure, no."

Victoria sided with Henry. "I think I'm inclined to agree with Henry here—this should not be our priority at this point. Let's give David some time and find out what he comes back with. But Henry: keep him on a tight leash. And Ron: if I find your fingerprints anywhere near this case, you will find yourself rotting in a French prison, US citizen or not."

Ron looked unsure whether Victoria actually was serious with her last remark, but he decided for now it was not worth testing it.

When Henry got back to his office, he found more bad news. A reporter who regularly wrote about agency business and was therefore under routine supervision had received an e-mail that contained details on the Minnesota bombing attack—three days before it happened! The e-mail scan had initially missed it due to the mail being dumped in the spam folder, but when she started asking questions about details that had not been disclosed in the case, people got suspicious and took a closer look at all her e-mail accounts.

Henry decided it was for now a simple case for the lawyers. They would file a lawsuit and slap a gag order on it citing national security constraints to make sure she could not publish anything. Then they'd force her to release her source. In the past this would have been seen as a horrible interference with freedom of the press. But since September 11, the FISA court routinely rubber-stamped requests like this, and he had no doubt that it would be the same this time.

If the lawsuit was not enough to make her see the light, they could always resort to other intimidation tactics, starting with a brief talk to her employer and people in her personal life. Or they might find financial or other improprieties that they could exploit against her. He was not really worried; leaks could easily be dealt with these days.

Ron wasn't in any mood to give up easily. Back at his office, his next call was to Dick Mulligan.

As David was driving back south with Erdal, a plan was forming in his head. He had to admit it was very risky, but if successful, it might put an end to this mess.

"How do you get in touch with your Russian friends?"

"What makes you think I have Russian friends?"

David chose not to answer and stayed quiet.

"Never directly. It's all through Hani."

"Since when?"

"They found me six months ago. Hani said they knew about our connection the moment I vanished five years ago, but it took them a while to find me. They also knew all this time that you were alive and that the assassination attempt was a con."

"Did they have a hand in it?"

"No. Imagine the FSB being caught assassinating a US government worker on US soil. Even the most concrete-headed

KGB spooks are horrified at that. They say it was an inside job. Part of a fight for direction in the agency."

"What is the FSB's direction these days?"

"Same thing. There are the traditionalists like Yuri who have been sidelined for a while. And then you have the Young Turks who think they can do better than just gather intelligence. They manufacture the news so that it fits the story they'd like to tell."

"Propaganda always used to be part of the KGB's duties."

"Yes, but they had always been pretty clear internally which was which. Now it's different."

David thought Ron the Hun would feel quite at home there. "So which side decided to bring Snowden in to Russia?"

"Neither. They both opposed it. But apparently politics felt like they had to take him. It left the FSB with a bit of a dilemma. It's not like they are any more civilized than the NSA and CIA. They just haven't been caught yet."

"I take it your contacts are part of the traditionalist faction?"

"They despise the new movement. Like most of us who have real work to do, they say it's hard enough to distill reality from all the misinformation in the world. The last thing they need is an added layer that makes the world look the way we'd like to see it."

"I might have something that could help them and help me."

"You're thinking about switching sides?"

"Not a chance. But I think this craziness has to stop, and I'm willing to take some risks to make it happen."

"What do you need?"

"A meeting with Hani and possibly his boss."

"Not good. They will try to bring you in."

"I'm pretty good at evading capture. I think you just saw that."

"These guys are different—very methodical."

"I have no choice."

"Then I will set it up."

LANGLEY, RON'S OFFICE.

Dick Mulligan never liked being called into Ron's office. It usually meant that he was asked to do things he thought were on the border of being illegal and sometimes well across the border. Plus, he liked to at least pretend he had some authority, but Ron treated people as if they only existed to do a single job and after that they could be dumped somewhere until he needed them again.

Ron came right to the point: "So have you found Nicole Monthausser yet?"

"We have traced her steps to Toronto, then Paris."

"Who was with her?"

"She was alone when she crossed the border to Canada."

"Why wasn't she stopped there?"

"She was traveling on a valid Dutch passport that we issued for her. There was no reason to restrict her travels."

"There is one now. I want to know when she crosses the next border. Can we revoke her passport?"

"I'm afraid not. It's not our jurisdiction."

"Who the fuck set this up?"

Mulligan decided not to answer.

"Never mind. So how do we find her now?"

"We spoke to her closest friends in Syracuse. Nobody knew anything except for one person who said she asked him to cover for her to get an extension on some assignment."

"What's his story?"

"Former boyfriend. He says she told him she needed a break and was planning to see a concert in Toronto and was hoping to meet up with some friends from Switzerland."

"Does any of this pan out?"

"She did buy tickets for the concert. We found plenty of people from Switzerland flying into Toronto airport around this time. Even when narrowing the candidates to her age group, there were over four hundred matches. Cross-referencing for possible past contact got us nothing so far. But more importantly, we have her in Paris the next morning." He waited to let this sink in.

Ron didn't get it. "Meaning what?"

"She had no intention of going to that concert. She drove straight to the airport and got the next available flight."

Ron raised an eyebrow. "Go on."

"We can trace the path her phone took in Paris and afterward, and it did indeed travel toward the Swiss border. But it appears to have been stolen or otherwise changed ownership. The phone is in a town called Guebwiller in the Alsace right now. We asked French police for help under the pretense of looking for a person who is in the process of laundering money. They arrested whoever has the phone right now—it's a fifteen-year-old French boy who bought the phone for cheap on a street corner. They let him go and apologized."

"Any clues where the switch might have been made?"

"Almost certainly in Paris. The call patterns change there. First, the outgoing calls are for local numbers. Then, the phone travels eastward, and after that all the calls are within the Alsace region."

"Not sure what this means."

"Nicole didn't make any calls in Paris. We think the calls are all from new owners. However, she did look for the address of a restaurant. And we think she ditched the phone after she went there and possibly met someone."

"Any chance that someone was her father?"

"Only if he can be in two places at once. He was on the phone with Henry Fletcher at the same time, and we are able to confirm his location on a country road in the Alpes Maritime region just off the Mediterranean coast."

"Who else was at that restaurant then?"

"Unfortunately, it is a very busy neighborhood. We found lots of cell phones that were active at the same time. We are still working through the list to see if anything suspicious comes up."

"Whoever she met with probably has no interest in us finding out about them, right?"

"Possible. Why?"

"Have you checked for burner phones?"

"We have a few on our list. It's just that..."

"What? Those are the ones you need, right?"

"Yes, but there is not much we can do with them since we don't have any data on them."

"You can get the call detail records, can't you?"

"Still I'm not following."

"Once you know who they are in contact with, you can narrow down your contact list."

"Interesting. Might work."

Ron was rolling his eyes. *Might work? Why do they always send me the amateurs?* What upset him more, though, was that Mulligan was willing to spend all his time going through the phone records that were in all likelihood useless, rather than focusing on the likely candidates first. The one thing Ron couldn't stand was inefficiency.

"I will get back to you as soon as we know more."

"One more thing: Can you track her father's whereabouts while you are at it?"

"He is not in witness protection. You should talk to Henry Fletcher about that."

Ron was silently fuming, but for now there was nothing he could do.

When David checked his e-mail that evening, he noticed one from an e-mail account he did not recognize: pyrenee.farm@gmail.com. No subject line. He was tempted to ignore it, but someone clearly knew something about him. When he clicked, he realized immediately where it came from despite the fact that no name was given. All it said was, "Nice job this morning. Watch out—he's furious." He figured there was no point in responding—he'd thank Angela later.

He also knew it was time to send a follow-up to Judith Ingersson, the reporter in Minneapolis. He went through the same routine as last time to mask his identity and location. Then he created a fresh temporary e-mail account and started with the subject line "Don't Delete: This Is Another Three-Day Notice." He explained his expectation that his credentials were by now established. Then he went on to describe the next terror plot to be "uncovered."

He hit the send button and was ready to reverse his tracks to delete all his temporary accounts when his e-mail client showed a new message in his inbox: "Don't Delete Me Either: Read First."

David was a little surprised to get a response that quickly and opened the mail. It was asking him to suggest any mechanism for a two-way communication so that Judith could ask him questions. Otherwise she would not be able to publish any of his material. He thought for a minute, then decided to type a quick reply: "Sorry, not possible. I'm not asking for publication. Strictly background. Watch out—mail will be monitored."

With that he signed off and was now in a hurry to wipe his tracks.

NEXT MORNING, MINNEAPOLIS.

Judith's editor at her local paper was usually easygoing and left her a lot of latitude to research any story she thought was worth going after. He only asked that she send him material on a regular basis and bring in some big fish at least once or twice a year. So far this arrangement had worked great for both, which is why Judith was a little surprised about this morning's phone call.

"What are you working on right now?"

"A couple of stories. Why, do you need anything specific for the paper this week?"

"No, just walk me through what you have brewing."

Not an unusual request from most editors, but given their working relationship it was still a little odd, Judith thought. But she walked him through the three stories she was actively pursuing and decided to leave out the big one that had not really formed in her head yet.

When she was done, there was a brief moment of silence on the phone, then, "Which one of these do you think would attract the attention of Homeland Security?"

Now Judith had a hunch. "None. Meet me for lunch?"

"Can you at least give me an idea?"

"Not on the phone."

"Barrio at noon?"

"See you there." Judith wished he had not mentioned the name of the restaurant. Was she getting paranoid? Hardly surprising given the nature of the two e-mails she had received last night. Then again, noon was only an hour away. If anybody would want to listen in on their conversation, they'd have to be pretty quick on their feet.

She arrived at Barrio a few minutes early. Al, her editor, was already there. Before she sat down, she took out her phone and gestured to him to hand over his phone. She took both of them to the bartender who knew the routine and put both in his freezer until they were done with their conversation. Ever since she read about Edward Snowden's revelations about how the NSA was able to listen in to almost anything they chose by simply turning on the microphones on people's phones, she had started taking serious precautions. And in this case she figured it wouldn't even count as paranoid since they almost certainly would be interested in what she had to say.

"Glad you came. Don't you think the spy routine is a little over the top?"

"Wait until you hear."

"Me first. I need you to stop digging into whatever it is that you are working on."

"Excuse me?" In her entire career, she had never heard anything like this.

"Judith, I'm serious. I had a visit from two gentlemen from Homeland Security this morning. They delivered a court order that prevents us from running any stories about terrorism that you plan on filing. It also comes with a gag order that prevents us from even talking about the fact that we received such a court order. I'm probably violating it right now."

"Then aren't you glad I froze your phone?"

"This is not funny. What the hell are you up to?"

"Are you seriously telling me you'll just fold?"

"No. The lawyers are fighting this, of course. But it could take years, and given how the government is cracking down on leaks, the last thing I need is to be in the middle of this. As much as I'd like to fight this battle, we are not the *New York Times* and we do not have their resources."

"So I should take it to the *Times*?"

"You should stop what you are doing. Leaking confidential government information is illegal, and people are going to jail for it."

"I have not asked anybody to leak confidential information."

"But you have received it?"

"I honestly don't know. If what I received is true, though, then the problem is not so much confidentiality as it is evidence of the worst government corruption we have ever seen in this country."

"Then let the lawyers take a look."

"There is not enough for them to look at."

"Okay. I probably should not ask, but what is it?"

Judith filled him in.

"You are predicting that in three days the San Francisco police are going to find a stash of explosives in a local mosque and arrest five members of the mosque for planning to plant a car bomb in rush-hour traffic on the Oakland bridge?"

"Yes."

"And you know this today?"

"Yes."

"So they have a tip and they are watching them. Not that unusual for police."

"Not a tip. I have the exact weight of the explosives, the manufacturer, and the serial numbers of the blast caps. If this were a tip, how could all this be known?"

"Do you realize what kind of accusation you are making here?"

"Of course I do."

"How reliable is your source?"

"I have received a previous tip-off, which I ignored. It was about the Bloomington bombing. I knew about it three days ahead of time, same as now."

"You knew about the mall bombing before it happened? Why didn't you call the police?"

"Because it looked like one of the many crackpot e-mails I get every day. Except it had all the details: identity of the attackers, size and weight of the bomb, even the license plate of the car."

"License plates are usually not even publicized in a case like this."

"I called John to verify."

"Wow. I'm speechless."

"So was he. I think he realized immediately what it meant."

"You are playing a very dangerous game."

"It's not my game. I didn't volunteer for this."

"So how did this guy find you?"

"I have no clue. E-mail showed up out of the blue. He deletes the account when he is done sending. The e-mail header indicates that it is routed through one of those anonymizer networks, so there is no way to figure out where it is coming from."

"Who do you think it is?"

"Someone on the inside who thinks this is reprehensible and wants it exposed."

"Which explains why Homeland Security is showing up with a leak investigation."

"I suppose."

"They have asked for all related material to be turned over to them so that they can trace the material back to the source."

"No chance."

"Judith, are you willing to go to jail for this?"

"Do you remember the case at the *Times*? Judith Miller refused to disclose the source of her leak. She had one big advantage: at least she knew who it was. I don't even know who my informer is. I couldn't disclose anything even if I wanted to."

"Which is why there is no harm in simply handing them everything you have and letting them figure it out."

"Except we disclose what we know, and we set a precedent for letting the government snoop around in our sources—in a case where the source is accusing the government of egregious misconduct. Over my dead body. I am appalled that you even suggest it."

"I have no doubt that they already know about the content of your e-mail. They all but hinted at it. And as far as the precedent, I suspect they will force us."

"Then they will have to use force, and we will get publicity out of it. The least we can do is make them look like a bunch of fascist storm troopers."

"The people I spoke to earlier aren't storm troopers; they are simply doing their jobs. But I'm sure they will tell you their story in person, if they haven't yet."

"Great, really looking forward to that one."

"Judith, I'm sorry, but you could have chosen gardening instead of national security as your specialty."

"I suppose I still can. Or maybe I become the Martha Stewart of design tips for your prison cell. Based on what you're telling me, that's where it seems to be heading."

"I wouldn't look at it that bleakly just yet."

The conversation with her editor had rattled Judith more than she thought it would. She always figured something like this would happen sooner or later. But so quickly? How could they possibly know so fast? She had not written a single word yet. Or was it really true that they saw each and every e-mail? It appeared to be worse than even George Orwell could have predicted.

Hani had suggested meeting in Nice. David liked the idea of meeting in a crowded area, but wasn't too thrilled about Nice because he didn't know the city well enough. They agreed instead to meet at the yacht marina at the Croisette in Cannes. It was reasonably crowded, but also easy enough to walk out onto the quay without raising suspicion and keep any possible access point in your field of vision.

When David arrived, there was no sign of Hani. He walked past the cafés and shops and then turned onto the narrow rock pier that served as a mooring station for some of the most expensive boats in the world. As he passed the first row, he saw that Hani had arrived.

"Pleasure to meet you. It appears we have a long history together."

Hani smiled and said, "That's right, and from what I'm hearing we might extend our business for a while?"

"I would think that the best thing for everybody might be a quick transaction."

"Oh?"

"Look, I think we all know what's going on here. I'm not about to defect." Hani looked in the direction of the boat rental office, and David, following his gaze, figured he had some people parked there. "What I have might be far more valuable than just another double agent."

"We were hoping for a straight conversion. We would evacuate you, give you a safe place to stay, and make things as comfortable for you as we can."

"Sorry if that was the impression you had. But I am not a Kim Philby case. I'm here to propose something else. And in case you were wondering, you can call off the two guards at the rental office; same for the two down at the real estate office at the other end of the pier. Have you noticed the police presence around here? They received an anonymous phone call this morning that someone might try to steal one of the boats. So they are watching the area very carefully. All I have to do is create some noise around one of the expensive boats and the gendarmerie will be here, ready to arrest you and me on what will turn out to be nothing but a misunderstanding on my part."

"Okay then. Your rules. What do you have to propose?"

"I have printed out everything you need. Take a close look at this file. At this point I have two choices available to me: I can either expose the entire operation and it will leave a ton of rotten egg on everybody's face including the FSB's. Or I can expose only the key player on the agency's side by making him look like a foreign agent. The latter is clearly the option with less damage for everybody, but it would require some cooperation on your end. I'm hoping that it serves your needs as well."

"Some people in our line of work call this blackmail."

"And others call it horse trading."

Hani smiled. "Personally, I like the second option. But I have to run it by some people, as you would expect. Where can I reach you?"

"I know how to find you."

Hani raised an eyebrow. "If you mean through Erdal, he might not be available much longer. We have plans for him."

"I figured. That's why I traced his movements. You're still staying at the Rue Parmentier address for a while? Nice views across the hills up there."

Hani was clearly not pleased. But he said, "I will be waiting for your next message."

"How did it go?"

"As planned. When were you going to tell me about your imminent departure?"

"I had no other choice. You were out of the picture, and the only person I knew and trusted was Hani. I had a hunch early on that he was with the Russians, and when he came to confront me about your role, I knew I was stuck—the only way to keep my cover was with Hani's help."

"I understand. But there is pretty intense pressure for me to bring you to Langley. You can either let me do that or run quickly. If you choose the latter option, all I ask is that you do it in a way that doesn't come back to me."

"We have already moved out of the ski condo. Once the French police look at the case, it will seem that I moved straight from Hyeres to a Russian safe house in Draguignan. And David: thank you. I would have preferred to keep working with you."

"I know. Me too."

LANGLEY, RON'S OFFICE.

Bill Mulligan wasn't sure whether the news he had was good or bad, and given Ron's reputation for instant temper tantrums, he wasn't too thrilled walking into his office with the thin amount of news.

"See, the problem is we found a pretty large number of phones that were set up without an account in the various neighborhoods in question. The largest cluster was at a restaurant on an island in the Seine River. We think this is the most likely place where Nicole's original phone changed owners. The call patterns afterward show nothing but local numbers. Looking at the cluster of phones there at the time, we ruled out some candidates quickly—they were prepaid phones but the accounts have been refilled at regular intervals, in most cases with a credit card or bank card that can be traced back to what looks like the phone's owner."

"And the rest?"

"There were a few that were brand-new, and their accounts have been filled with cash payments, which we consider a strong indication of them being used as a burner phone. Three of them look like they traveled together from Paris to a town called Béziers, about halfway between Montpellier and Perpignan, not too far from the Spanish border. They are still there."

"Good work. Thank you." Ron was reasonably certain this meant David had found someone to pick up Nicole and to stay with her. The question was how to deal with it since he had just promised Victoria he'd stay out of this.

The station chief in Montpellier was mainly concerned with French industrial conglomerates in the region that had a reputation of competing with their American counterparts and enlisting French intelligence services to keep a leg up when bidding on projects. Airbus in Toulouse was his biggest target. He was about to analyze a transcript indicating that Airbus knew about Boeing trying to undercut their pricing for Emirate Airways and had to make a decision whether to hand over this information to his friends in Seattle when he received a call from headquarters.

"How quickly can you assemble a field team in your area? I would need about four to five agents for an extraction. We can't use diplomatic channels. I'm thinking instead that having someone transported with a freight container might work."

"We don't normally do this kind of work. This is mostly a listening post."

"You'll have to make an exception."

"I'd have to engage some freelance people we have used occasionally. Would that work?"

Ron didn't like it, but also knew any other option would take far too long in this case, so he answered, "I think it will do. I don't expect resistance or anything."

"Where is the target?"

"Two people staying in the Hotel Imperator in a town called Béziers. Room number 108 on the first floor above the lobby. I will arrange for transportation. Have everybody ready and on standby tomorrow morning. I will send you the details about the target in a few minutes."

This was clearly outside his regular line of work, but the station chief decided to treat it as an opportunity to show what he was capable of. He hoped it might give him a chance to be transferred to a posting that was less of a sleepy backwater than his current one.

"One more thing: you will need to make sure there is no trace of this, even internally."

"Not a problem." It was actually a bit of a problem since his budget was tight and he needed to find a way to pay his freelancers under some account where it would not be questioned.

Chapter 10

David didn't get to check his e-mail until late at night when he picked up another mail from Angela with a single sentence, asking, "What are you doing in Béziers?" He decided this was reason enough to call her immediately.

"I'm not in Béziers. Why are you asking?"

"Your friend has arranged outgoing transport from there."

"Are you sure?"

"Container in the cargo hold with oxygen supply to support two large, sedated animals is what it says on the request."

"He's trying to ship two people to the US without going through official channels?"

"That's how I read it."

"Anything else?"

"His phone record says he was on the phone with Montpellier."

"Only industrial intelligence these days."

"Probably all he could get. He's officially grounded and won't be able to go himself."

"If you can see his phone records, he can see yours, right? Be very careful."

"You know I'm the master of deleting trails."

As soon as he got off the phone with Angela, David tried to reach Nora but her phone was off and it did not have voice mail set up. He considered driving to Béziers, but it would have required changing his next steps with Hani. Instead, he left a message with the hotel and asked them to write a note for her that simply stated "call your friend" and slip it under the door. He would try her phone again in the morning.

"Ron, we have a problem."

"Only one? What is it?"

"You asked me to set up traps to make sure we know when someone checks on your activity. Someone just looked at your transport request."

"But it doesn't have any specifics in it."

"Enough to draw conclusions. Everybody knows we are not in the business of transporting large animals."

"Who was it?"

"Someone smart enough to wipe their trails immediately. But not smart enough for me. It was someone in Henry's SigInt department."

"You have a name?"

"Not yet, but it shouldn't take long."

"Do we still have access to the farm near Gaithersburg?"

"Yes. Why?"

"Once you know who it is, bring them straight there and make sure the interrogation equipment is ready."

"Ron, are you sure about this? We are talking agency personnel here."

"Actually, we are talking traitors."

"Which is when we normally call in the FBI."

"You trust the bureau with anything besides pushing paper? Come on."

Ron had a point. Officially, the FBI was in charge of monitoring and counteracting foreign agents, but they had not been very good at it in recent years. Most people inside the agency would rather mount their own counterintelligence than trust their colleagues at the bureau. Yet, this felt wrong—it did not feel like a foreign agent, more like interoffice squabbles. But there was no arguing with Ron, not for people who wanted to keep their jobs.

Angela was in a good mood when she left the office. Whatever Ron was up to, she felt pretty sure that she had thrown a wrench in it. She unlocked her car and was ready to drive to her gym to get an hour or two of workout before meeting her mother for dinner.

"Hello, Angela."

She had never seen the person who just popped up in her backseat holding a gun. This was the agency parking lot and no sane carjacker would try anything this stupid here. Then again, what carjacker is sane to begin with?

"We are taking a little detour. You'll have to give me a lift to Gaithersburg."

"Why would I do that?"

"Because I'm holding a gun and because someone wants to talk to you."

"Talk."

"Yes, just talk. Don't worry. You'll be on your way in no time."

She worried all right. There was only one reason someone might want to talk to her at this time and with the kind of urgency that requires a gun being pointed at her.

The extraction team was ready and on standby in Montpellier early in the morning. It was made up of French nationals who had done various jobs for the agency in the past. As soon as they had the go-ahead from headquarters, they'd be on the road. The call came in at 7:00 a.m.

David had gotten up at six to call Nora's cell again. No answer. He tried again at seven with the same result. At 7:30 she finally picked up.

"You need to leave. Right now."

"What's going on?"

"Destroy your electronic trail, and get on the road. Don't use your car. Find a different way."

"Next steps?"

"Improvise."

"What do I need to watch for?"

"Extraction team sent by the Montpellier office."

"Size?"

"Unknown."

"Time?"

"Likely already on the way."

Nora noticed the piece of paper under the door. "'Call your friend.' I assume that means you?"

"Yes. Your phone was off."

"Sorry. Gotta run."

"Let me talk to Nicole real quick."

"Dad? What's going on?"

"Nora will tell you the details. You need to get out and listen to her. I will meet you as soon as I can. I love you."

"I love you, too. Is this going to end soon?"

"I promise it will."

After he hung up, David thought about what else he could do. His options were limited, but there was one possibility. He picked up the phone again.

"Hello, Jean."

"Who is this?"

"It's been a while. I was supposed to be dead."

"David? Mon dieu."

"Listen, I don't have much time. Are you still in charge of southeastern France?"

"Nothing ever changes here."

"Béziers is part of your territory?"

"Sure is."

"The agency is trying to extract some people from there."

"And you need us to help?"

"No. I would like you to prevent it."

After a moment of silence, Jean Renard said, "You are asking me to interfere with your agency's activity?"

"It's complicated. I think it is not an officially sanctioned action. I do not have time to look into the details, but I definitely don't want to clean up after it—would much rather stop it before it happens."

Jean had never liked the fact that other countries seemed to treat his territory as fair game for their spying activities, and it didn't take a lot to convince him to disrupt them whenever he could. In the past he had been a thorn in David's side often enough, but eventually they developed a cordial relationship and respected each other's boundaries as much as it was possible given the nature of their business.

"Our closest office is in Montpellier. How quickly is this happening?"

"Might be too far. What about the local gendarmerie?"

"Not sure if I would trust them once people are wielding guns."

"There might be no other choice."

"I'll see what I can do. Where is everything happening?"

"Do you know the hotel Imperator?"

"I know it well. Lousy location for an abduction."

David was relieved to hear that.

Nora had crushed their cell phones and flushed them down the toilet. Normally she would have preferred to drop them into somebody's passing car or find some other way to set a false trail, but she did not think she had the time to do that. They were walking down the large staircase when she noticed two people at the front desk who looked like they could be the cousins of Yuri's pit bulls. When she saw two more outside the front entrance checking the sidewalks, she knew it was time to turn around. She grabbed Nicole's arm, turned her around, and ran up the stairs to the top floor.

"What now?"

"First some instructions on what happens if they catch us since this seems very likely at this point."

Nora ran Nicole through her standard advice. Don't resist. If they hit you, relax your muscles to soften the blow. Never hit back. Make sure you have air to breathe. Don't scream unless you are sure someone can hear you.

"This is frightening. You really think we are not going to make it out of this? Do you not have a plan B?"

"I'm working on plan B. Come with me."

She knocked on doors, hoping someone would open. They got lucky after the third attempt. Nora pushed the door open. It was an elderly man in his underwear.

"Monsieur, please call the police. The hotel is being attacked by a group of robbers."

Aside from a shocked expression on the man's face, she could not tell whether he understood. He showed no sign of doing anything about it. So Nora picked up the phone herself.

"No dial tone. They cut the lines."

She looked around and saw the hotel's brochure sitting on the desk. She turned it over; it was white in the back. The drawer had a pen and she wrote on the back, "CALL POLICE. ROBBERY." Then she walked over to open the window, hoping someone in the office on the other side of the street would be able to see her. But it was not even 8:00 a.m. and nobody had arrived at work early.

"Nicole, grab this." She pointed at the desk, and together they lifted it away from the wall and brought it toward the window. "Does it fit?"

"What do you mean?"

"I think we can get it through."

"What?"

"We need to attract someone's attention."

They lifted the desk through the open window and let it drop from the fourth floor onto the street, which resulted in a loud crash and quite some yelling by people who almost got hit.

Nora held her sign out the window and yelled down at the same time hoping someone would take her seriously and call the police. Then she retreated inside, grabbed Nora, and said, "Time to move. I'm sure they noticed where this came from."

They ran down the hall toward a door marked as an emergency exit. The door led to a staircase onto the roof.

"This will be the first place they will check, so it won't work for too long."

They waited tucked behind one of the electrical closets up on the roof listening to doors opening and closing at various ends of the rooftop and hoping for the police sirens to start. Nicole thought it took an eternity until they finally heard the sound they were desperately waiting for.

At the hotel's entrance, police cars pulled up and gendarmes ran into the lobby with weapons drawn. They went from floor to floor to check whether any rooms had been burglarized. The only room with any unusual activity was the one that had a desk missing and a very distraught elderly man who claimed two strangers had come in, tried to use the telephone, and then dropped his desk out the window and ran away.

Police Captain Rene Bardet was ready to call it over and check it off as one of the peculiarities that happened in his town, when he received a call on the police radio from the DCRI asking to talk to the person in charge.

"Who is this?"

"Jean Renard from the DCRI office in Aix-en-Provence."

"It's a pleasure, but things are a bit busy here—we had a call about a break-in."

"Hotel Imperator?"

"How the hell did you know?"

"It's not a break-in. It's an attempted abduction. You are looking for four or five men, likely armed and dangerous. In addition, two young women—they are the victims in this. I'd like you to bring everybody into your office. I will be there as soon as I can."

"We are just about done going through every room of the hotel. We found no signs of anybody."

Jean Renard thought about this information for a minute. Any chance David was wrong about the location? "Ask the front desk whether their phones are working."

Bardet came back on the radio almost immediately. "Lines are cut."

"Have you checked the basement, the roof, the parking garage, and other areas that are accessible from the hotel?"

"No. We were called about a burglary. When we saw no signs of one, we figured false alarm."

"False only as in false advertising. It's a kidnapping, not a burglary. You better keep looking and find those bastards or I'll have your ass."

Bardet knew this was no empty threat. The DCRI was in charge of all domestic counterintelligence and counterterrorism operations, and they had a reputation of having a very short fuse. He stopped his officers who had just wrapped up their activities and told them to surround the hotel, bring in more backup, and go floor to floor again, but this time look for every exit door and check what is behind it, not leaving out the roof, the basement, the parking garage, and any connections to neighboring buildings. In the meantime, he was looking around for cars parked close by. He figured whoever was trying to pull this off would have to keep an escape vehicle not too far from the entrance. He found a Peugeot van pretty quickly with a nervous driver inside and the engine running.

About ten minutes later, the team on the roof requested assistance over the radio. It had encountered resistance from at least two armed men. Another ten minutes later, it was all over. They had four armed thugs and one driver in custody. Two frightened looking women were sitting in the lobby trying to explain what had happened. None of the explanations made any sense to Bardet, who was glad that in about an hour he would dump this whole mess on Monsieur Renard from the DCRI.

Renard called back David on the number he had left.

"We have five thugs and the two women in custody. I will be driving to Béziers. Can you meet me there?"

"I have to be in Nice today. Can I meet you tonight or tomorrow?"

"That's fine. I will have to straighten out this mess anyway. Any more information you can give me about who is who?"

"One of the women is my daughter, Nicole. You might remember her from her baby pictures. The other is a woman who had volunteered to stay with her and keep her out of trouble."

"One of yours?"

"Not really. Random acquaintance."

Renard's instinct was impeccable. "Which service?"

"Israeli. Don't give her a hard time. All she did was help."

"They are not supposed to be here."

David knew Jean had a nasty run-in with a Mossad group earlier in his career and was generally suspicious of their intentions. "Look, she was here to meet with me and stuck around when I asked her to help Nicole. I had nobody else to turn to."

"What on earth did you get yourself involved in?" Renard started to suspect David might have just tricked him into taking sides against the CIA and did not like it one bit.

"Don't worry. I'm still on the right side of things. I will explain when we meet."

"This better be good."

"Oh, it is."

When David turned on the local news, reports on a kidnapping interrupted by local police in Béziers was top of the news. Nicole and Nora's faces were shown along with the five men who kept their heads down as far as they could for the cameras. He hoped against his better judgment that it would take a while before this reached the other side of the Atlantic. By 6:00 a.m. DC time (noon in France), Henry had gotten wind of it and called him.

"I think I just saw your daughter's face on TV. What the hell have you put her up to? And don't feed me the 'it was my idea to put her into witness protection' line again. We both know this is bull."

"I just heard from Renard. He is on top of it and will figure out what happened."

"You're trying to say you don't know?"

"All I know so far is that someone in the agency sent an extraction team through the Montpellier office. I do not know whether they were hoping to find me like last time we met or were going after Nicole."

The hint about the last botched kidnapping did the trick. "Montpellier hasn't done this kind of work in many years."

"I know."

"Renard is involved?"

"He just called me. He's on his way to Béziers."

"I will get to the bottom of this. One more question: Have you heard from Angela?"

"Angela? Why?"

"She is always here bright and early. She has not shown up today."

"Is Ron there?"

"Just ran into him in the hallway. Why?"

"She was watching him. She thought he didn't know. But maybe he did."

"Dammit, David, did you fucking put her up to this? What else is going on?"

David figured he needed Henry's help on this one. "Henry, I swear I didn't ask her to do anything. Had she asked, I would have told her not to. But she called me late last night to say that Ron was planning some shady stuff in Béziers. I told her to be careful and not leave a trail. She thought she had her bases covered. But I suspect someone was watching her while she was watching."

"I am looking at the news as we speak. Who is the second woman?"

"I'm waiting to hear from Renard on that." He was hoping Renard would be careful enough not to talk to anybody at the agency; given his friend's natural inclinations he figured it was a pretty safe bet.

Chapter 11

His afternoon meeting with Hani went reasonably well.
Hani's boss still did not like the blackmail aspect, as he called it,
but getting out of the whole affair with nothing but a black eye
seemed like a pretty good deal especially if it meant getting a
chance to blame everything on the radical faction in the FSB.

David had his next move lined up. He sent an e-mail to Judith Ingersson using the exact same method he had used before. Except this time he copied Dan Frederickson at the FBI.
He had worked with Dan a few times and knew he would not
take the content of this e-mail as lightly as some others might.
He again received an instant response from Judith. This time it
said, "I'm under pressure not to publish anything. My paper received a FISA gag order."

He responded, "No surprise. I suspect it only covers topics I
had written about in the past? Don't worry—they were not
meant for publication, just to establish my credentials. This one
you should be able to run with. Call Dan Frederickson at the
FBI." Then he wrapped up his trail and left for Béziers.

He called Jean Renard from the road to find out what was
going on.

"Man, this is quite the hornet's nest you had me poke into."

"Why, what happened?"

"Diplomatic personnel running all over this. American embassy calling. Israelis getting involved. All I need is the Russians and we can start having a fucking peace conference down
here."

"Any of them creating real trouble for you?"

Jean Renard sounded as if he might even enjoy the excitement so far. "Only yours. They are trying everything they can to
get your daughter turned over to them. I told them I have nobody here called Nicole Monthausser, all I have is a Dutch citizen called Erica van Wyden, one unidentified non-EU citizen
who does not fit the description, and five French nationals, all

with criminal records. So I didn't see any reason for them to have jurisdiction over anybody."

"Where is she?"

"Right now still answering tedious questions by the local cops. They wanted to put her up in a hotel in Montpellier, but I think I will take her home with me instead, if you don't mind. You want to meet me at my house for dinner? I have a nice bottle of Côtes de Provence waiting to get out of my basement."

David was thrilled, and not just because of the shorter drive—Aix was about 150 miles closer to Nice than Béziers. More importantly, it solved another much bigger problem of keeping Nicole and himself out of reach of a second attempt. He did not think anybody was crazy enough to send a team to the private home of the regional head of the DCRI.

David had just pulled into Jean Renard's street when his phone rang.

"David, it's Henry."

"What's going on?"

"Quite the entertainment you are providing for us here."

"What did I do?"

"Cut the crap, man. Nice job getting the thugs arrested that Ron sent."

"Trust me, I had absolutely nothing to do with that. I was in Nice when I heard about it."

"Whatever. I expect Nicole is with you by now?"

"No, but I hope I will meet her in an hour or so."

"The French are making quite a stink about this. They called our ambassador into the foreign minister's residence for a severe beating. And they have already announced to the press that they will kick out the station chief in Montpellier and our head of operations in Paris."

"I thought everybody involved in this was French?"

"Except that the driver was stupid enough to keep all the paperwork in the glove compartment. Phone numbers. Instructions given to them by Montpellier. Contacts to call when the job was done. And most important, shipping instructions to Andrews."

"Is this some joke? They couldn't find anybody competent? Jesus Christ."

"It gets worse. Your buddy Renard has already connected this whole thing with last week's embarrassment in Mulhouse. Now the French are saying we are manufacturing passports claiming diplomatic immunity for people who are not supposed to have it."

"Are they wrong?"

"You know it doesn't matter. The problem is they are now asking for extradition of some key personnel who have violated French laws. Top of the list is one Ron Polanyi."

"Ron the Hun in trouble with the law. I'm shocked to hear that."

"Don't be so smug. If any of this is traced back to you, people will be asking for your head."

"Sounds like you are having an interesting start of the day."

"None of this would be a reason to call you."

"So what is it?"

"Angela is missing."

David felt a knot forming in his stomach. He did not know what to say.

"She did not show up this morning. I called her cell, her home, no answer. I know she frequently checks in with her sick mother, so I called to see when she last spoke to her. Her mother says Angela didn't show up for dinner last night. She was already in a panic—she says Angela is never even late."

"She would never drop an appointment with her mother without calling and letting her know. Her mother is the one constant in her life."

"So I traced her cell phone, and it is somewhere outside Indianapolis. Turns out someone put it on a truck that is going cross-country."

"Lousy news. What does Ron have to say?"

"Can't touch him. He's being read the riot act by the AD for having violated her direct order to not go near you or anybody connected with your case. Right now you could ask him whether it's raining and he would refuse to comment without his lawyer."

"I have a case?"

"David, there is a lot to explain. But not now."

"I have an hour before I meet Renard."

"I don't. But we do need to talk. Where can I find you tomorrow?"

"Aix-en-Provence. You know the Forum des Cardeurs? There is a café on top of the hill. I think it's called Café des Cardeurs. I'll be sitting outside, right next to the old well."

"I will see you tomorrow morning. Say hi to the old grouch Renard for me."

"I think I can tell you right now what his answer will be— say hi to that redneck Fletcher."

"Well then, tomorrow morning at the thistle café—fitting location for thorny topics."

"Carders are not thistles. I don't think they have thorns either. But nasty weeds they are indeed. See you tomorrow."

David saw Renard pulling up to the house and got out of his car. Nicole yanked open the passenger door before Renard had a chance to stop, jumped out, and ran toward him. "I am so glad to see you. Dad, what the hell is going on?"

David hugged his daughter tight. He knew she had to be frightened and looking for answers, but after five years of not seeing her, he felt nothing but overjoyed.

"Dad, you're crying."

"I know. Sorry about this mess. Come, I have a lot to explain I suppose."

Renard jumped in, "To me as well. But I can wait. Looks like you two have some work to do first."

"Speaking of work. There is one thing I need to check very quickly, if both of you don't mind."

Renard gave him a quizzical look. "Related to this case?"

"I'm not sure. It's a loose end that I just heard about, and if it is related, it would be very bad news."

"You'll let me know?"

"If it affects you, absolutely."

David logged into the agency network knowing that he was violating security protocol by using Renard's Wi-Fi connection, which was probably routed through DCRI headquarters and subject to cryptanalysis there. But this was urgent.

He looked through Ron's activity log and was not surprised to find nothing of interest—it had been wiped clean. He thought for a minute about the minimum requirement for Ron to pull something like this off. Abducting agency personnel would be a point of no return, even for him—even if he had some sort of cover story. If such a story existed, he had to manufacture it somehow. And he would need access to a secure location. Despite what people read in spy novels, safe houses are actually very rarely used, and, especially on domestic soil, there are only a few. He decided to search backward and find out which safe houses had been requested recently and for what reason.

He had only two candidates. One had been requested for a Chinese national who was expected to defect while on assignment in DC. The other was a farmhouse in Gaithersburg, Maryland, set up for interrogation. It was checked out the day before for questioning of a member of a Syrian rebel organization with links to the Islamic State of Iraq and Syria, also known as the Caliphate. The request for Gaithersburg had been canceled five minutes after it was made. David knew that it was not possible to make a request vanish once it was submitted. The next best thing was to mark it as canceled so that it looked like a mistake. He suspected this was Ron trying to clean up after himself. He sent an e-mail to Henry, asking whether Ron's cell phone trace showed any trips to Gaithersburg. Then he logged off to join his host.

Jean Renard stopped him in the hallway where the others would not hear them. "I had no idea you could do this."

"Do what?"

"Check people's activity log."

"You were watching?"

"The DCRI runs routine session and keystroke logging for every connection that goes through its network."

"And you were watching me."

"Only because I'm worried."

"To answer your question, I'm not supposed to. But remember, I work in SigInt."

"What's with the Syrian stuff?"

"Just a hunch. A friend of mine is missing. I suspect it may have to do with retaliation for helping me."

"Henry Fletcher is involved?"

"He says hi, by the way. Only involved in the sense of trying to get this mess straightened out. He will be here tomorrow morning."

"How is the old redneck?"

"Same old. Ask him yourself tomorrow."

"We do have a network in Syria, in case you need help."

"Too early to tell."

"You still owe me an account of what the hell you got yourself into."

"Then I might as well tell you over dinner since Nicole deserves the same explanation."

With that, they joined Nicole and Jean's wife for dinner and the bottle of Côtes de Provence, which turned out to be three bottles before the evening was done.

David gave the best account he could about what had happened during the last few weeks, adding some pieces for Jean's benefit about where he spent the last five years. He knew what he had to report did not help to calm Nicole's worries.

Jean noticed the same thing. Turning to her, he said, "You know, hearing all this, I am actually very glad you ended up staying here. I don't think there is a safer place for you anywhere in Europe tonight."

Nicole smiled but then said, "What about Nora?"

"Oh, they will have some stern questions for her tonight. But as far as I can tell she has not committed any crimes unless you want to count throwing a heavy desk out of a fourth-floor window, for which she will have to pay. So by tomorrow morning, my friends in the gendarmerie will see no reason to hold her. They will call me to see whether there is any national security interest. I will shrug and say 'to hell with her.' After that she will be on her way to Israel."

"Will I see her one more time? We got off on the wrong foot, but I'd like to thank her for what she has done to help me."

"Depends on her. She might want to get out as fast as she can before we change our minds."

"I don't think she will be in a hurry." David was pretty sure Nora was not done yet. "Is there any reason you'd expel her, or could she stay if she chose to?"

"That's not really up to me. You think she has things left to do?"

David wasn't sure how much to tell Jean. "She was looking for people when I met her. I'm not sure that she found them yet."

"This wouldn't by any chance have to do with some Chechen thugs burning down a house in Hyeres and leaving from a nearby airfield before we could catch up with them?"

"Is there anything that you don't notice?"

"Plenty. But not if it happens in the South of France. Keep in mind that people in the tax auditor's department are talking to my people all the time. Nicely done by the way. We almost overlooked it. So who was the person the Chechens were after?"

"One of my former informants. He hasn't been active in five years, though."

Jean raised an eyebrow. "I thought the only inactive agency informants were the dead ones, no? Either way, where was he hiding after the Chechens were done with him?"

"Draguignan as far as I know."

"That apartment was a cover. We have him taking a bus from Valberg to Nice. That's pretty far from Draguignan, wouldn't you say? Have you ever been skiing up there? It's gorgeous—lots of red limestone canyons, and the slopes are spectacular."

David held Jean's stare. "Elana's sister used to have an apartment there. She might still come here in the winter, but I have not spoken to her in the last five years."

"Interesting coincidence."

Next morning David and Jean were waiting at the Café des Cardeurs for Henry to arrive. Over the coffee bar, a TV was showing the news. Yesterday's excitement in a provincial hotel was almost forgotten, now commanding only some questions about why the CIA was trying to abduct a young Dutch woman from French soil. A spokesman for the French president was quoted with an announcement that the responsible CIA employees had diplomatic immunity but that they were not welcome in France and would be expected to leave the country within twenty-four hours. The Dutch government called in the American ambassador in Den Haag to let him know how utterly outrageous it was to attempt to kidnap a Dutch citizen on European soil. David almost felt sorry for his agency to see how much rotten egg was piled on its face.

The next part of the news seemed completely unrelated. According to a Minneapolis newspaper and confirmed by sources in the FBI, an unnamed CIA agent had been accused of spying for the Russian FSB, the successor of the KGB. Russian sources were quoted with a tight-lipped "no comment," which news analysts interpreted as the Russian way of saying "so what?" They also suggested an exchange for Americans working for nonprofit organizations in Russia who had been convicted of supporting the Russian opposition parties—according to the analysts further proof that the Russians were ready to accept the accusations as real and were eager to get their man released.

Henry joined them while the news about the CIA mole was still running. "Quite a mess, I'd say."

"Quite so."

"Jean, I'm sorry my colleagues have left this chaos for you. I will do my best to help clean it up."

"Oh, don't worry. The whole affair has helped us find a bunch of thugs who belong behind bars anyway. I assume you're not here to bail them out?"

"No way; put them where they belong. If you need any help on that, let me know. I will share whatever I can."

"Thank you. This sounds unusually cooperative."

"We'd rather get past it. This should have never happened."

"You're not suggesting we should stop spying on each other?"

"I wouldn't go that far or I might be out of a job. But committing violent crimes and trying to abduct Dutch citizens from a foreign country can't possibly be part of my job."

"Glad you see it that way."

"But I have an urgent problem that I need to talk to David about, if you don't mind."

David volunteered, "he knows about Angela."

Henry was stunned. "How?"

"When I checked on the Gaithersburg stuff, I had tunneled in through a DCRI network."

"David! Weren't you the one who always said—"

"I know. Look, it doesn't matter; we can use all the help we can get, right?"

Jean added, "Even if it's just to have another set of eyes, I'd be glad to help."

Henry didn't like it but he kept talking. "We checked Gaithersburg. There was some very ugly stuff happening there. We found blood and plenty of evidence of someone having been tortured there. But no sign of Angela. We are analyzing the blood to see whether it is hers. More importantly, we found a flight to Syria yesterday morning. It was a transport marked as a terrorist transfer. Ron claims he has no knowledge of anything but that he thinks there is evidence that Angela was part of a sleeper cell connected to a group called 'Free Syrian Islamic Jihad' or something like that."

"What a pile of crap."

"We all know that, but it looks like he covered his tracks pretty well. He seems to have manipulated her communication records to make it look like she was in contact with the Syrian group. He also knew about some local imam in DC who is supposed to be the leader of the sleeper cell. Angela's phone has called him three times in the last two months."

"Any idea where the flight was taking her?"

"Tall Rifat. A small town outside Aleppo, not far from the Turkish border."

"And the group is known to be active there?"

"Yes."

"So he sold her out as a prisoner to some Islamic nut cases."

"We don't know that, David."

"But we can find out."

"How?"

"I met someone yesterday who would be able to tell us who is who in Syria."

Henry frowned. "Friendly?"

"No. But reasonable."

"When can we go see him?"

"We can't. I can."

"David..."

"Seriously, Henry. If you show up, we get nothing. We need this."

"You are emotionally involved."

"Damn right I am."

"Then you need to stay out of it."

"Try and make me."

Jean found the right words. "What do we hope to gain from this contact you met yesterday for the first time?"

"A read on who is behind this group in Syria."

"I might be able to do that for you. Remember, we have long-standing relations, and we still have pretty good contacts on the ground there. Let me make a quick call."

While Renard was on the phone, Henry filled David in on the details of what was going on in Langley. Ron had indeed been arrested by the FBI on charges of espionage. Victoria was furious. She was still trying to figure out how the FBI was tipped off about Ron's Russian connection without her knowing anything. State Department was on their case for ruining relationships with friendly allies. Everything was a complete mess.

Jean had bad news. "My friends in our foreign department were laughing at me. Your Free Syrian Islamic Jihad is your own front for supplying arms to rebel forces. They take money and hardware from the CIA, most of it is channeled through the Saudis and the Emirates."

David was confused. "If it's ours, how can there be a sleeper cell?"

"There isn't. Someone is feeding you cow manure. But they must have known this would not remain hidden. So if your friend is really on her way to Syria, the question is where did they really ship her to? I doubt they kept her with the group that was named, right?"

Henry was pretty sure: "If it's ours, I will be able to find out."

And it was Henry's turn to get on the phone. In the meantime, Jean turned to David. "You're close to this missing lady?"

"Somewhat."

"Sounds like all your women are getting in trouble these days."

"Not funny."

Henry came back with the news. "It is our own group. They said they were supposed to receive a prisoner yesterday, but the shipment never arrived. According to their story, the prisoner was a member of an Islamic fundamentalist group called Jund al-Aksa."

"Who sent the prisoner?"

"One of Ron's cronies did. But here's the problem. They think the plane actually landed and the prisoner was handed over, but not to them."

"Then to who?"

"Jund al-Aksa."

"Shit."

Jean said, "Let's get back to my house first. By now your friend should have arrived."

They found Nora talking with Nicole in the Renards' living room.

David turned right to Nora. "What do you know about a group called Jund al-Aksa?"

"Fundamental Islamic, your usual brain-dead, anti-Israel, guns-and-Koran outfit. Why?"

"We think they are holding one of ours."

"Not for long then."

"What do you mean?"

"If they know he's yours, he won't be alive for much longer than a day or two."

"We are not sure if they know. But it's a she."

"Then the outlook is even bleaker."

David turned pale. "What do you expect to happen?"

"Close friend of yours?"

"Yes." His face turned red now.

"I'm sorry."

"I gotta go." David was getting ready to walk out. Henry was trying to hold him back, but David brushed him off and said, "Look, I didn't choose to create this mess. But I will not let people get hurt just because they are close to me. Not this time."

He got into his car and was ready to drive when Nora opened the passenger door. "Wait. I can help you navigate this mess. Please."

"Get in."

They arrived at the Rue Parmentier in Nice just before 1:00 p.m. Hani answered the door. "Come in. Who is she?"

"Hani, I'm sorry to disturb you. This has nothing to do with what we had talked about earlier. Everything is in motion and appears to be running well. Thank you for your help with every-thing."

"So then why are you here? And why did you bring more people into this?" Hani was alarmed. No good could possibly come from any continued contact.

"I have a big problem. Someone who has helped me in these last few weeks has been caught and sent to Syria."

"Not a good vacation spot right now."

"Does the name Jund al-Aksa ring a bell?"

Hani tried not to give any indication that he recognized the name, but David knew better. "Your friend got caught by them?"

"That's the rumor I heard."

"And you want me to confirm or deny."

"I was hoping that you had some connection that would help track her down."

"Her? Are you serious?"

"Why?"

"This group is worse than the Taliban. How did your friend even get there?"

"We think she was sent directly by the CIA."

Hani shook his head. "And you believe it?"

"I have nothing else to go on."

"When did this happen?"

"Yesterday morning local time."

"Any details about your friend?"

David rattled off Angela's full description: five foot eight, close to 150 pounds, dark brown shoulder-length hair, brown eyes, pale skin, narrow face, high cheekbones, straight nose, slightly slumping shoulders.

"Give me a minute."

Hani went out of the room to make a phone call. When he came back, his face was even more severe than before. "They do not have her. But they know about her."

"What does that mean?"

"The people I just spoke to are in a town called Tall Rifat in northern Syria. They are colocated with a group that is a CIA front. They use some generic name that's supposed to sound like they are fighting the Syrian government."

"We know about them."

"My contact says your shipment indeed arrived yesterday morning. It went to the CIA portion of the camp, and the Jund al-Aksa people were a bit appalled by the whole affair. First of all they object to the presence of women on a battlefield on principle. They think it's wrong, that it will corrupt the fighters. But they are also devout Muslims, and they don't like it when people get tortured. They say your friend was subjected to more pain than anybody should have been—and that says a lot coming from these people."

David could barely speak. "Is she still there?"

"The camp came under attack from government forces yesterday. Your CIA group jumped ship quickly. Normally they would have cleaned up, killed your friend, and then destroyed any evidence. But it seems they either didn't have time or thought she was dead anyway. Whatever it was, they just left her and ran. The government forces weren't really interested in her either and ignored her. So after they moved out, Jund al-Aksa took control of the town again and found her still alive."

Nora mentioned, "If they still have her, we could probably get an extraction team ready."

"They did not keep her. They do not have the capacity to deal with a situation like this. They put her on a convoy of fugitives headed for the Turkish border. And that's all they know."

"Hani...thank you. I owe you."

"You don't. There's a lot of nasty stuff we do in our business. But there is no need to lose all civilized behavior."

Nora said, "If she's across the border in Turkey, I have some people who can find her."

David thought about it for a minute, then said, "That would be great. I need to wrap up one more thing with Henry, then I'm ready to go wherever you tell me in Turkey."

When they got back to Jean Renard's house, Henry was on the phone. Apparently, the situation in Washington had gotten a bit tense over revelations that Ron the Hun had not acted alone. Victoria insisted that Henry came back immediately to help clean up and deal with damage control.

"Can we have a quick word first?"

"On the way to the airport."

"Okay."

Once they got into the car, David got straight to the point. "I know you think I'm ready to defect."

"I didn't say that."

"Truth is every agency around the world would like me to. And sometimes I think even ours would prefer that outcome."

"I need you to help me with the aftermath of this disaster."

"We both know this is a bad idea. Ron might be gone, but there are plenty of little Rons running around the agency floors. They will all be out for blood."

"Even more of a reason for you to stay."

"I'd have a big bull's-eye painted on my back."

"Nothing you can't handle."

"True, but I don't want to. I have seen my daughter dragged into this, and I have had enough. I am retiring just like you wanted me to five years ago."

"Why do you think this would work? You said so yourself many times: there are no retired agents unless they are dead."

"I have created my own insurance policy. In the last few weeks I found all the details in our archives about how the agency manipulated the public perception of the threat potential. Every little detail about the Anderssen Gambit is ready and prepared for public consumption. When published, it will have a far worse effect than the Snowden disaster or any other of the past leaks. Plus, with everything that has been revealed so far, people will actually believe it."

"Where will you be when this hits the fan?"

"I'll be dead."

"I don't think I understand."

"But you do know how a deadman's switch works, right?"

"You spring-load a mechanical trigger, and as long as someone holds it down, nothing blows. You kill the person holding the switch and the bomb goes off."

"Right. And if you translate this to a digital world, you have a mechanism that checks regularly for my continued existence and well-being. If it gets no answer from me, it goes into publication mode."

"Except nobody will print anything without getting answers from you."

"Why do you think I need anybody's help to print? It's the age of social media—everybody self-publishes. This is no different. Plus, you should know that I have no problem getting text into major mainstream publications bypassing any editorial control. Hell, even you know how to do that."

"So you are blackmailing me."

"No. I'm ensuring my undisturbed retirement. You and the agency will leave me and my family alone and nothing will happen. You mess with us, the world will know about all your dirty tricks."

"And the world believes you rather than us?"

"I think you had a taste of it already."

"So you were behind the leaks in Minnesota."

"I didn't say that. And I'm not the only one who can figure out what is going on. If you want my advice, you'll change the way the agency works. And then you gradually own up to what happened in the past. It's the only way to defuse a bomb like this one."

"Many people at the agency would disagree."

"And you'll have your work cut out to get rid of them one by one."

"What happens if you die of natural causes?"

"The switch doesn't care. Neither do I. Which is why you should get your act together and clean up the agency so that it is no longer a big deal when the last details become known. I may have another thirty years or so, but nobody lives forever."

"That's a tall order."

"Who told you first that running the Anderssen Gambit was a lousy idea?"

"I didn't run it."

"But you own it now."

Henry didn't look happy. But David knew he had gotten his attention.

"Safe travels."

"Thanks. Watch yourself. You are playing a dangerous game. There are people who might think you are bluffing."

"They are in for a nasty surprise then."

Before he went back to Jean Renard's house, David made one quick phone call. This time Bromberger picked up the phone himself.

"I think you can start putting pressure on the agency now."

"What do you mean?"

"It took me a while to understand what your real game plan was. Clearly you didn't need me to figure out how the Anderssen Gambit was being played. You had all the access to find out the details yourself. You needed me to get the agency into a state where it would be receptive to pressure from politics. So tell your friends it's time to start using their influence."

"I'm impressed. We should work with you on a regular basis."

"I am not available. The last thing I need is regular trouble like this."

"Fair enough. One more thing: I hear you might need a ride to Turkey? One of our team members has a private plane waiting at a small airport outside Aix. We figured it was the least we could do."

"Thank you. For everything."

Epilogue

Markus Bromberger wasn't looking forward to the meeting he was about to have. He knew this person as one of the most manipulative people he had ever met and preferred not to talk to him.

"Mr. Bromberger! Come in. Have a seat. I hear you have done a great job with this little assignment we gave you."

"Thanks, Mr. Secretary. I didn't really do much. I only relayed the information to people who needed to know."

"Usually, this is all it takes. So I hear Mr. Polanyi confessed to having spied for the Russians? Do you believe him?"

"I think, if it's true, it's probably the least of his crimes."

"Spoken like a true diplomat. Ron was always a very misguided individual. And much too ambitious for his own good. Always ready to jump to conclusions. When we were looking for information about nuclear weapons in Iraq back in 2003, it was because we thought there was a chance that they existed. Ron took it as an assignment to manufacture proof of their existence, if real proof couldn't be found. The problem is he probably thought he was fully in sync with myself and the former vice president. He could not be more misguided."

Bromberger almost felt sorry for Ron—clearly he had been manipulated into thinking he was acting in the interest of his sponsors and now he was being dropped like a hot potato. Bromberger was wondering whether the same fate was waiting for him some time down the road. Aloud he said, "It seems like he was pretty convinced that he was doing the right thing."

"Aren't we all? But I wanted to ask your opinion about David Monthausser. You watched him up close, didn't you?"

"I only met him twice. But he seems like a well-grounded guy."

"I heard he is somehow blackmailing us now?"

"Not really. He did precisely what we expected him to do. He just took it a tiny bit further by forcing the agency to clean up its act. I think it is actually good for the agency because sooner or later some of this will definitely leak."

"Only if he wants it to."

"No, too many people know about it. Somebody will talk."

"So you think he is really acting in the best interest of the agency? That's an interesting thought."

"I do. I think he is a true patriot—he had every chance to defect and profit from what he knows. But he chose to stay loyal and help clean things up."

"I don't like it when our reputation gets smeared."

"And I think he would wholeheartedly agree. But he is also realist enough to know that we can only control the messaging to some extent. He wants to make sure we get in front of the news rather than cleaning up after it."

"So you think we could use him again in the future?"

Bromberger thought for a while. Then he said, "I'm sure we can."

"Whatever happened to the girl who got mixed up in this whole thing?"

"She is still recovering in one of our military hospitals in Germany. It looks like she might make a full recovery."

"Then it seems like it all ended well, didn't it?"

"Most people would say so."

Stay in Touch

Stay connected with the work of BJ Pascal at http://www.-monthausserfiles.com or follow him on Facebook (https://www.facebook.com/pages/BJ-Pascal/1485558125054058) or Twitter (@bjpascal).

www.ingramcontent.com/pod-product-compliance
Lightning Source LLC
Chambersburg PA
CBHW060643260626
47161CB00008B/2979